THE DARK
SHINES BRIGHT

THE DARK SHINES BRIGHT

Written & Cover Designed by:

RICHARD A. HENRY

ARPress
45 Dan Road Suite 5
Canton MA 02021

Hotline: 1(888) 821-0229
Fax: 1(508) 545-7580

Ordering Information:

Quantity sales. Special discounts are available on quantity purchases by corporations, associations, and others. For details, contact the publisher at the address above.

Printed in the United States of America.

ISBN-13:   Paperback   979-8-89389-784-5
              eBook   979-8-89389-786-9
              Hardback   979-8-89389-785-2

Library of Congress Control Number: 2024923096

CONTENTS

CHAPTER ONE

It was a glorious spring day in Ramsey, New York. The kind of day that makes you feel great just being alive, able to savor the warmth and fresh air. With the deep blue sky for a backdrop, the brilliant sun radiated through the fluffy white clouds, and increased in brilliancy with each note the birds chirped of what sounded like a song of happiness and life.

But the beauty of the sky went unobserved, and the angelic chirping of the birds went unheard by the two dozen or so people who stood in silence, their heads bowed in reverence, as they listened to the words of the minister. "Remember man and woman that thou art dust and to dust thou shall one day return. Let no man or woman mourn the passing of Mildred Marshall, for hers was a good life and she is now receiving her reward in heaven."

Almost simultaneously with the words 'reward in heaven' came a cold, chilling wind that swept through the entire cemetery. In conjunction with the wind's arrival, the clouds, which seconds earlier were bright white and scattered throughout the blue sky, turned an ugly gray. They clustered together, eclipsing the sun and blackening the sky. The birds stopped singing and darkness engulfed the entire area surrounding the cemetery. There was a long moment of vacuum like silence that was finally broken by the sound of trembling earth. A streaking bolt of lightning followed the shaking immediately. As the powerful thunderbolt flashed toward earth, it split in two, striking the earth at the base of the headstones to the left and right of Mildred's casket, cracking each headstone into two equal parts.

As mysteriously as the strange atmospheric occurrences began, they dissipated. The trembling of the earth ceased. The clouds returned to a bright white, while simultaneously breaking apart to allow the sun's rays to touch the earth again. The birds reappeared in the once again bright, blue skies singing louder than before.

The mourners stood in dismay staring at the cracked headstones for a few seconds before slowly turning toward one another. Everyone was seeking reassurances that they had actually witnessed the eerie events. Except for the split headstones, everything was just as it had been sixty seconds earlier. The mourners began to chatter amongst themselves, until the minister's voice rang out again. "As we return Mildred's body to the earth from whence it came, let us remember that one day we too shall return to the earth."

The ceremony ended without any additional interruptions. After the last mourner gently placed a yellow rose on top of Mildred's casket, those who came to pay their last respects began to disperse. As they returned to their cars, almost everyone was engaged in various conversations. There wasn't the normal talk that followed a funeral and burial. No one was talking about how special a person Mildred was, how she was going to be missed, or how sorry he or she felt for Paul. Instead, the talks centered on the strange occurrences of twenty minutes earlier. In a small town such as Ramsey, there would be talk of Mildred Marshall's funeral for years to come.

The ride home was a long, lonely one for Paul Marshall, as he sat alone in the rear of the lead limousine. His head was buried in his hands, and his large six foot-two, one hundred and ninety-pound frame seemed much smaller as he sat bent forward in anguish. He sobbed in silence. Paul had loved Mildred more than he loved life itself. Every since he first met her she had been his driving force. Now she was no longer with him, and his dreams of all that he had wanted out of life seemed to die with her.

Paul began nervously tugging at his thick, black and gray mustache as the limousine slowly rolled along Main Street. He raised his head and stared out the tinted windows. The familiar sights seemed to cut into him like the sharp edge of a fresh razor blade. There was the Village Park where he and Mildred went on their first picnic when he was a young man of twenty-one, just out of college. He had big plans for his family's lumber business. He was going to build it into one of the largest corporations in the world. Few who knew him doubted that he wouldn't succeed. He had finished in the top ten percent of his graduating class at Ramsey High. His academic success continued in college. Besides making the dean's list all four years, he had been an outstanding football player. Several sportscasters billed him as one of the best running backs in his conference. After graduation, Paul turned down several offers to turn pro. He felt that the sooner he returned home, the quicker he could begin to build Marshall's Lumber Yards into the corporate giant he envisioned it becoming.

Paul and Mildred met the week after he graduated from college at the annual Ramsey fair and charity bazaar. Mildred's father had recently accepted a professorship at the State College ten miles north of town. It was love at first sight for Paul, when his eyes caught a glance of Mildred standing with a group of other young women. She was smiling and laughing at something one of the women had just said.

When Paul saw her smile for the first time he thought, 'My God, standing just feet from me is the most beautiful woman I have ever seen.' Mildred's smile caused him to feel as though he was suddenly on an endless elevator ride, dropping faster and faster, suddenly stopping, then dropping and stopping again, over and over. Suddenly, Mildred turned toward him. When they made eye contact for the first time, the motion in Paul's stomach stopped, and a lump began to rise from his stomach to his throat where it sat.

As Paul stared at Mildred, the sun cast its rays on her fiery, red hair giving the appearance of a halo perched ever so gently upon it. Her eyes, which were a bright, light brown, appeared even brighter as the sunlight bounced off them. 'God, she's beautiful,' Paul thought again, as he stood mesmerized, lost in instant fantasies of being with her. He was so enveloped by his thoughts that he hadn't noticed her walking toward him.

"Hi. How are you?"

The sudden sound of her voice caused Paul to jump and snap out of his trance like state. Standing less than four feet in front of him was the woman of his dreams

"I'm Mildred and you are?"

Paul cleared the lump from his throat while fighting to

regain his composure. "Paul, Paul Marshall," he replied nervously.

The two of them stood staring intensely into each other's eyes, as if they were paralyzed, for what seemed like eternity. They were falling deeper and deeper in love with each passing moment. Their ecstasy was interrupted by the sound of several approaching people. No more words were spoken immediately, but it was evident that true love had found them and that they were meant to spend the rest of their lives' together.

'Yes, this red head, brown eyed gift from God is the woman I want; the woman I need in my life,' were Paul's immediate thoughts.

Mildred's thoughts were similar. She had never felt like this before, and she never wanted to feel like it again, unless it was with Paul. For the remainder of the summer they spent nearly every free moment they had together.

Paul proposed to Mildred in late August that very same year. She accepted without hesitation. They set a wedding date for the last Saturday in September. The wedding was the largest ever held in Ramsey. Almost the entire village was present. It was clear to everyone at the wedding that Paul and Mildred were bound together by a deep, profound love.

The next thirty years saw their love grow stronger with each passing day. It grew with the joy of the birth of their only child, Anthony, a year later. It grew even stronger as they shared the happiness of watching him grow up, bringing them closer and closer together. It grew through the tragedies of life as well. Such as the sudden and unexpected death of Mildred's father from a heart attack; the death of Paul's parents in an auto crash on Good Friday twenty years earlier;

and their biggest tragedy in life until that time; the death of their son in a distant place named Vietnam.

On the surface, Paul seemed to take the death of their only child a lot harder than did Mildred. He had spent the past twenty-five years laboring hard to realize the achievement of his dream. Marshall's Lumber Yards, under his leadership, had become one of the world's largest conglomerates with corporate headquarters in New York City, and operations in several countries around the world. Paul looked forward to being able to pass the reigns of what was now called Marshall Enterprises International Inc., to his son. He looked forward to an early retirement, and enjoying the fruits of his labor with Mildred. He always gave her full credit for being the driving force behind all his achievements in life.

A big part of Paul's dreams were shattered a few years earlier by the ringing of chimes one, cold, dreary, winter morning. No words were necessary when Paul opened the door, and saw the United States Marine Corps Captain and Staff Sergeant standing there. As always, Mildred was his pillar of strength in difficult and trying times throughout their entire lives together. She always rose above the pain of her own suffering and comforted Paul in his moments of need whenever they arose. If she were not there by his side, he would not have been able to survive the almost unbearable heartbreak and pain than he experienced having part of his lift's dream so abruptly snatched from him when he received the news of his son's death.

Paul's thoughts of the past were interrupted as the limousine turned into the long, winding driveway, and came to a stop in front of the row of white steps leading to his front door. The driver quickly stepped from the car and opened the rear door. Paul emerged ever so slowly. He pulled himself our of the car by clutching onto the roof with both hands, then stood outside the limo with his arm resting atop it for support. Paul felt as if the weight of the world was suddenly bearing down on him. He glared at the mansion that he and Mildred turned into a home full of warmth and love. Whenever he returned from one of his frequent business trips, his heart would swell as he approached the door, for he knew that once inside he would be with his love and partner for life.

Today was different. Paul knew that beyond the door there would be no one to greet him, except the servants. The mansion seemed to have lost the warm feeling that once had been ever present. It now seemed like nothing more than a huge structure made of stone and marble. The windows looked like dozens of eyes staring coldly at him. The door seemed like a giant mouth waiting to swallow him. For the first time in his life, he was almost afraid to enter his home.

It took Paul a few minutes to pull it together before he could force himself to begin slowly climbing the steps. His heart felt the pain of Mildred's death more and more, as each step he took drew him closer and closer to the huge, wooden, double, oak doors. Just as he reached the top step, the butler opened the doors. Paul stood at the entrance staring inside. The house no longer felt the same. He stood there with one foot inside the foyer for a few seconds before entering. Once inside, he took off his coat, and handed it to the butler. There was no need for them to exchanged words. The Marshall's long-time servant knew there was nothing he could say that would help ease the pain. Paul knew that he understood his suffering.

The next several hours seemed an eternity to Paul as he listened repeatedly to the countless, repetitious condolences from those who came to offer their sympathy. The parting of the last person who came to express their sympathies around seven p.m. couldn't come soon enough for Paul. Their words and gestures meant nothing to him. He neither wanted their sympathy nor needed it. What he wanted and needed was for Mildred to be there to console him, just as she always had been in the past.

Shortly after the last mourner left, Paul seated himself on the sofa in the family room. He began reminiscing about the countless evenings spent with Mildred by his side engaging in many meaningful conversations and hearty laughter, while sharing their love and the warmth emitting from the fireplace.

Paul continued to sit in silence for several hours, barely moving, lost in his innermost thoughts while the servants cleaned up. When they finished, Elizabeth, the head housekeeper interrupted Paul to let him know that the cleaning was complete, and then asked if she could be of any further help.

"No. I'm fine," Paul replied. He thanked Elizabeth for her help, and asked her to extend his thanks to the rest of the household staff. He then informed Elizabeth that he needed to be alone, and that she and the rest of the staff could have the next few days off. Shortly after that, the staff was gone and Paul was alone.

A few minutes later, Paul slowly stood up and strolled to the bar that sat off to the right of the large, oval room. He reached into the ice bucket, took out several ice cubes, and dropped them into a glass. He then filled the glass almost to the top with rum, topped it off with a splash of coke, climbed onto a barstool and began to drink.

His thoughts drifted to County General Hospital, room 666, where just weeks earlier Mildred lay dying of a brain tumor. Contrary to superstitious beliefs and other dark connotations usually associated with triple-six, the three-digit number had always been what he thought to be a lucky one for him. He met Mildred on the sixth day of June, around six p.m. Their son was born on the sixth day of the month, and his house number was 666 Gemini Lane. He even had custom plates on his car with the numbers 666 inscribed on them. Paul had always been a deeply religious man, and as Mildred lay dying, he prayed to God, asking Him to save her. He hoped with all his might that triple-six would come through again, and that in spite of what the doctors told him, Mildred would pull through in room 666.

Day after day, as Mildred grew closer and closer to death, Paul continued praying. He begged God to allow her to live. He pleaded with God to take his life instead of hers. Please, just let her live. His prayers and pleas were in vain. He refilled his now empty glass, while he continued to think. What type of god have I been worshiping all my life? What type of god would ignore me when I needed his help the most? What a fool I've been for worshiping a god who probably doesn't even exist. If in fact there is a god, he must be a vain, vicious thing who created and destroyed life for personal enjoyment. His anger continued to mount. Finally, he decided he no longer wanted a part of such a cruel and heartless god.

Paul spent the next several hours thinking of the past and the countless, happy times he shared with Mildred over the years. After finishing three quarters of the bottle of rum, he exited the family room, walked down the long hallway, stumbled up the steps, and entered the master bedroom, which he and Mildred had shared for so long. He was now totally inebriated from the numerous rum and cokes he consumed. He was barely able to make it across the room to the bed. Within minutes of falling onto the bed, he was fast asleep. Sleep brought Paul a temporary reprieve from his pain and suffering.

CHAPTER TWO

Paul awoke early the next morning. Lacking any incentive or desire to get out of bed, he just laid there looking around the room. 'Mildred you had such great taste for decorating,' was just one of his thoughts as his eyes focused on the furnishings in the room. He looked to the far end of the room and continued reminiscing. He couldn't count the times he would awaken bright and early in the morning to the sight of Mildred seated in one of the two white, wicker chairs in the room. They sat on each side of a matching wicker table, positioned between the two large bay windows in the wall opposite the bed. Mildred always called that small section of the bedroom her private, little nook in the house. The blue cushions, with their white floral design, matched the curtains covering the terrace door to the right. The floral centerpiece was a blend of various lifelike, silk flowers. Mildred would often get up an hour or so before Paul and sit there reading.

Paul continued scanning the room, slowly rotating his neck until his eyes reached the night table nearest him. His motion stopped as he caught sight of the pictures in the double frame that sat directly beneath the lamp on the table. The frame contained pictures of Mildred and their son,

Anthony. He remembered well the day the pictures were taken. It was the day Tony, as they affectionately called him, graduated from the United States Marine Corps Officers Candidate School at Quantico, Virginia. He looked so handsome standing there in his dress blue uniform with his new, glittering, gold bars. In the picture of Mildred, you could see the pride in her eyes that only a mother's eyes can reflect at witnessing her child's accomplishments. Paul looked at the two pictures side by side, and was reminded of how much Tony resembled his mother. Tears began to swell in the corner of his eyes. He quickly turned his head away, and buried it in the pillow. Eventually, he cried himself back to sleep.

When Paul awoke several hours later, he sat up in bed, and slowly looked around the room. There was something strange in the air. A sudden chill ran through his veins. The room seemed much too cold for this time of year. He shook his head and shoulders in a vain attempt to shake off the chill. It was at that point he first realized that what he was feeling was more than a chill. "What is it?" He asked himself aloud.

He continued trying to identify what he was feeling as he climbed out of bed, and glanced in the full-length mirror mounted on the closet door. "What a mess," he mumbled. He had fallen asleep fully clothed. His shirt, tie and trousers were full of wrinkles; his hair with its streaks of gray was disheveled. His eyes were swollen and red.

Paul stood looking at his mirrored image. He shook himself in an attempt to get rid of the unwanted, strange vibes that encompassed the room. The shaking was in vain. Suddenly, the feeling in the air that he awoke to seemed to intensify. Paul quickly turned away from the mirror, and looked around the room expecting to see someone standing there. There was no one physically in the room, but there definitely was a presence, if not in the bedroom, somewhere in the house. He stood motionless, feeling a little nervous for a few seconds before setting out to explore where the presence was coming from.

Suddenly, without warning, something seemed to take control of Paul. He found himself guided to the bedroom door by an irresistible force. When he reached the door, he hesitated, while trying to regain control of himself. He couldn't. Pauls' forward motion continued to be controlled by the force that now seemed to govern his every movement. He was being led unwillingly into the hall, down the steps, through the foyer and into the kitchen toward the door leading to the basement. Just as he reached the large door, a piercing wind raged through the house, sending books, lamps, ashtrays, pictures, trophies and furniture into the walls and onto the floors, shattering all that was breakable. The powerful gush of wind headed straight for the partially opened, cellar door and slammed against it, wedging it shut.

Still controlled by the force that led him to the door, Paul extended his arms, wrapped both hands tightly around the large, shinny, brass doorknob and tried to open it. It quickly became apparent to him that whatever caused the wind to shut the door, whatever force led him to it, was unquestionably stronger than any strength he could muster. The more he struggled to open the door, the tighter it seemed to wedge shut. After struggling with the door for a few moments, Paul released his grip on the knob. Once he released his hold, the force that had led him to the door seemed to almost simultaneously release its grip on him.

Paul stood there motionless. He was aware that a force beyond his control had led him to the cellar door. "But why?" he muttered. His fear began to mount as he continued to ask himself questions. "Where did the wind come from?" It bore with it the same chill that the equally mysterious wind that interrupted Mildred's burial services the day before carried.

Before Paul could begin to try to rationalize what was occurring, his thoughts were quickly disrupted as a light of blinding intensity appeared at the top of the door. Paul raised his hands in an attempt to shield his eyes from the light, which had begun to encircle the door. It was losing more and more of its brilliance as it surrounded the doorframe.

Once the circle was completed, the now dim light seemed as though it was about to disappear, when suddenly, the circle burst into hundreds of rings of color. The rings shot in every direction, passing through objects and the walls of the house. Then, with such fury that it shook the entire house, shattering several windows, the basement door flung open.

Paul stood paralyzed by fear as his eyes fell on the eerie figure standing at the top of the steps leading to the darkened basement below. Before him stood a creature that he thought existed only in the world of nightmares and science fiction. The entire red, lizard-like, scaly body before him was engulfed in flames, yet, the body itself, clearly was not burning.

Try as he might to put his entire body in motion, Paul found that he was only able to move his eyes. He began to look the silent figure over. At first glance, it appeared to be some type of creature from a prehistoric swamp. Paul continued to stare at the motionless figure. After gazing intensely for a few seconds, he realized that what stood before him was a creature that resembled a human being in almost every way except for its scaly, red skin and the vast wing-like structures on its back.

Both the silence and Paul's paralysis were broken by the sudden unexpected voice of the fiery figure. "Do not be afraid Paul Marshall, I have not come here to do you any harm. I have shown but a minute fraction of my powers. Had I intended to harm you, I surely would have done so by now."

Paul's first inclination was to flee, but he quickly rationalized that trying to flee would be pointless. It was more than obvious to him that what stood before him was some kind of creature that obviously possessed a great amount of power. Going against his basic instincts to flee or fight, Paul stood transfixed, staring wide-eyed as the creature continued to speak. "Several days ago Paul, your god dealt you a great injustice by taking Mildred's life. Yesterday, you thought you laid her soul to rest, but she rests not. There will be no rest for her. At least not until you strike back at your god for taking her from you. When you have done so, I promise you that you will join her in her new home in Hell. Only then will her tortured soul find peace with you by her side. You look surprised Paul. Maybe you expected her soul to be in the place your religion calls Heaven. My little show at the cemetery yesterday should have raised some questions in your Christian mind."

Paul's mouth dropped wide open as he attempted to speak, but was quickly silenced by the creature in front of him. "Speak not and listen, for when I'm finished you will have a clearer understanding of things. Above all, you will have a decision of great importance to make. I will start by correcting a few misgivings that most humans have about good and evil or God and the Devil. Think for a moment, if there were but one god and he was all good as your religion has taught you to believe, then there would be no opposite side to good. How could a god who is said to be all good and all powerful allow for the existence of evil and its seemingly constant triumph over good?" The creature continued to tell Paul the true story of the earth's creation and the reason for its existence.

"In the beginning there were two gods, not one as you have believed all your life. Both are equally all-powerful. The truth of the matter is that eventually they became bored with each other's company. To relieve their boredom, they decided to play a game. First, they created the universe and all that exists in it as their game board. Next, they created two powerful forces that you know as good and evil. They spread these two forces throughout the universe. When that was complete, they chose the earth as the starting point for the game. Then they created human beings to serve as the main game pieces. These players were given souls, which would serve as pieces by which the gods would keep score. When a human died, one god or the other collected their soul. Which one claimed the soul depended on whether the person's life was lived more by the forces of evil or the forces of good.

Initially, the rules of the game were simple. There was only one. That rule was, that once the game began, there would be no direct interference in the player's actions by either god. The game would end when the players finally destroyed themselves and the earth. Then the souls will be counted, a winner declared and a victory celebration held for all the players. At that point, the gods will decide whether they felt up to a new game that would begin elsewhere in the universe.

As with any game, the longer it lasted, the more the rules changed. Sometime they were simply ignored." The creature continued explaining how the game of the gods was no different.

"As the centuries passed, rules were added and subtracted by one god or the other. When one god seemed to be losing souls in disproportionately larger numbers to the other, changes in existing rules took place. Both gods have long since circumvented the basic rule of the game. At different times throughout history, each god has gotten around the rules by using various people as messengers, prophets or so-called leaders. There was David, Moses, Cleopatra, Caligula, Daddy Grace, Joan of Arc, Pope Gregory, Mussolini, Hitler, and an almost endless list of people who served unknowingly as agents of one god or the other."

The creature went on to explain how it too was an agent of the god whom humans called the Devil; the god who collected the souls of those who led their lives most influenced by the forces of evil. "Throughout history, often I have appeared to man on behalf of the Devil. History books make constant references to me, often describing me as a demon. I have come to accept the term as a way of being identified.

After what seemed like hours, but in reality had only been a few minutes, the demon stopped speaking. There was dead silence for the next minute or so as the demon stood glaring into Paul's eyes. Then in a slow, even voice, began speaking again. "I have spoken and you have listened patiently. Clearly you are wondering why I have appeared before you and how you fit into all that I have told you. Well Paul, it is really quite simple. There have been several people in the recent past who have, through their interfering in the lives of others, caused the Devil to be unjustly deprived of several souls destined to join him. Their interference has angered the Devil, and he has decided that they must pay by replacing the souls they caused him to lose with their own. To accomplish that Paul, an intermediary is needed. You are being presented with the opportunity to serve as that intermediary. That is if you want your dear, precious Mildred's soul to find peace, knowing that one-day you will be with her again. I have said all that I need to say, for now. The question is will you serve as an advocate of the Devil or will you turn your back on your dearly departed wife? Take a few of minutes and think well before you give me your answer Paul Marshall. I shall consider your word binding. Before you make your decision, I will tell you more about what will be expected of you. You'll have a few days to think it over."

The demon went on to provide Paul with a description of his mission and of the souls involved. One belonged to a Catholic priest. The second soul was that of a former Peace Corps worker. The third one belonged to the wife of an extremely powerful and very wealthy Senator/businessman. The demon went on to inform Paul that, as needed, it would reappear from time to time and give him further instructions. Most importantly, the demon let Paul know that he would be given certain powers to aid him in capturing these souls for the Devil. When the demon finally finished delivering his message, it took a deep breath, and slowly exhaled. Without saying another word the Demon vanished as quickly and as unceremoniously as it had appeared.

CHAPTER THREE

The sleek corporate jet came to a stop about two thirds of the way down the runway. At the far end, a chauffeur, who had been polishing a silver limousine, opened the trunk, threw the rag he had been using in, slammed the lid, and hurried into the driver's seat. He quickly sped down the runway toward the aircraft. When he reached it, he brought the limo to a stop a few feet to the left of where the craft had parked. At the same time, the jet's door swung open, and the steps were lowered. Paul emerged from his plane, and the chauffeur hurried over to greet him.

"Good morning Mr. Marshall. It's a pleasure seeing you again, sir. I'm very sorry about Mrs. Marshall," he continued.

Thanks, Brian. Everyone who was blessed to have known her will miss her. So, how are things in New York?"

"New York is still New York, sir. Would you be going home or to the office?"

"Neither. Before I do anything else this morning, I'd like to attend mass at a church uptown. Take the Grand Central to the BQE across the Fifty-ninth Street Bridge, Brian. I want a good look at that magnificent New York skyline."

Paul sat listing to the sounds the tires made as they skirted across the steel grading embedded in the bridge's concrete roadway. He peered out the windows; first through the left and then through the right. 'Sunday mornings seemed to give New York City a mystical air about it' was his immediate thought, as he continued scanning the skyline. The warm, June sun, reflecting in the skyscrapers gave the illusion that it was draped in a bright deep orange veil of silk. Manhattan seemed like a ghost town. Paul glanced at his watch. It was seven-thirty a.m. It's amazing, if it were Monday morning instead of Sunday morning, the streets would be filled with millions of people hurrying to work. That thought amused Paul as he continued to survey the nearly deserted streets.

There were only a handful of people walking on either side of Second Avenue. Paul looked up at the waiting room of the Roosevelt Island Tramway. It too was deserted, except for a young couple laughing as they stood waiting for the next tram. The man stood with one arm around the woman. His other arm had what appeared to be the Sunday newspapers tucked under it. Paul was always amused at how millions of people seemed to just disappear in New York at night and on weekend mornings. It was almost as if they had been magically whisked away. He always disliked having to fly into town on weekdays, even when business necessitated it. He never had any desires to trade the quiet, tranquil life of Ramsey. Being home provided him with a temporary and much needed escape from the everyday hustle and bustle that was characteristic of life in New York City. Since business matters often brought him to the city, he purchased a brownstone in the east seventies a few years back. He couldn't stand living out of hotels

Paul spent the next few minutes somewhat lost in his

thoughts. He interrupted them just long enough to address his driver. "Brian, when you get to Eighth Avenue, head uptown through the park. The church is on Ninety-seventh Street and Central Park West. When we get there, you can let me out front. You can take the rest of the day off. I'll catch a cab to the house later."

After giving his chauffeur explicit instructions, Paul leaned back in the plush seat and drifted again into thought. His thoughts, though many, all centered on one theme. 'Here I am, Paul Marshall, a mere mortal, and in my hands rested the fate of three souls.' Paul felt a surge of power flourish within.

Brian exited Central Park at Ninety-sixth Street, turned left, pulled the limo parallel to the curb and stopped. He got out, walked to the rear and opened the door.

"Are you sure that you'll won't be needing my services for the remainder of the day, Mr. Marshall?"

"I'm sure. You go on and enjoy yourself this fine day. I'll call you this evening to let you know what time to pick me up in the morning."

As his limo pulled away, Paul turned his immediate attention to the church. The last time he had been in a church was two months earlier for Mildred's funeral mass. He looked up at the massive church towers.

When he completed scanning the towers and the remainder of the church's exterior, Paul climbed the steps leading to the large, studded, brass doors of St. Aloysius Church. They were propped open to let in the cool morning air. Paul strolled past them and entered the vestibule, where he proceeded to undergo the familiar symbolic Catholic rituals. Having attended Catholic school from the first through the eighth grades, and having been a devout, practicing Catholic all his adult life, the motions were almost second nature to him. He dipped his right, index finger in the dish of holy water, by the side of the entrance and made a quick sign of the cross. In the past, it had meaning; now he just went through the motions purely out of habit.

Paul took his time heading down the center aisle, looking the entire church over as he went. He had never been in Saint Aloysius before. It was a beautiful structure. It appeared to have more stained glass windows than other Catholic churches he had visited in the past. Even the cathedral ceilings seemed higher up than the ones in the other churches. To the right and left of the main altar were smaller ones. A shrine of The Blessed Virgin Mary was next to the left altar. The one to the right had a shrine to Saint Joseph. In front of each shrine, there were six rows of offering candles, and a metal box for donations. Paul reached the entrance to the first row of pews, genuflected and entered the pew on the left. He glanced at his watch. "Seven-fifty, ten minutes before mass starts," he whispered to himself.

Paul continued looking around the church. When his eyes fell upon the confessional booths in the rear of the church, he laughed to himself. He noticed that the line in front of one confessional booth was a lot longer than the other. He remembered his childhood days at parochial school. The word was out which priest was the best one to hear your confession; he handed out fewer repetitious Hail Mary's.

Paul's train of thought was broken by the sound of footsteps on the center altar. He quickly turned his attention to the priest who was carefully placing a set of chalices on the altar. He calculatingly followed the priests' every movement as he walked off the altar, turned back to it, genuflected and made the sign of the cross before returning to the sanctuary. He recognized the priest immediately from a description provided by the demon. He was, after all, the reason for his being there.

The activities in the sanctuary were like those of any other Catholic Church on a Sunday morning. In a smaller room to the right, two altar boys hurriedly put on their vestments in preparation to assist with mass.

The Right Reverend Father John Carmeluchi stood in the dimly lit main room of the sanctuary, carefully adjusting his vestments. He was a tall, slender built man with a full head of gray hair that gave him a distinguished air of diplomacy. Once his garments were in place, Father Carmeluchi began to ready his chalice for mass. His hands shook, almost uncontrollably, as he dropped the unconsecrated hosts into the gold chalice. Seeing his hands shake made it difficult to believe that just a year earlier, Father Carmeluchi was often heard boasting of how, at sixty-nine years old, he had the steady hands of a man half his age. His friends blamed his current condition on old age and hard work finally catching up with him. He knew better. The good Father remembered all too clearly the day his hands first started shaking. It was a year ago to the day. He had just completed a successful exorcism, and when as he stood to leave the room, he felt a nervous twitching in his fingers. The twitching had grown progressively worse over the past year.

The priest's daydreaming was cut short when the altar boys entered the room. "Is everything ready?" he asked.

"Yes Father," they replied in unison.

"Good. I'll be ready in a few seconds." He handed the flasks containing the wine and water used in the service to one of the altar boys, who immediately went and placed them on a small table to the right of the altar. When the altar boy returned to the sanctuary, Father Carmeluchi looked at his watch. It was eight o'clock; time to begin the mass.

The altar boys were the first to exit from the sanctuary onto the altar. Upon entering, the one on the left reached up and pulled a chord, which rang a bell, signaling the beginning of mass. Father Carmeluchi followed them out of the sanctuary. When the congregation saw him, they stood. The procession of three slowly made its to the front of the altar. When they reached it, the altar boys knelt at the bottom of the first landing of steps, while Father Carmeluchi climbed the remainder of the steps. When he reached the top, he turned to the standing congregation and began mass.

Paul followed every movement the priest made during the service. Twenty-five minutes later, the mass ended. Father Carmeluchi faced the congregation, and bestowed his blessings. Immediately afterward, he and the altar boys disappeared back into the sanctuary. After the service, Paul hung around outside the church a little while where he picked up parts of various conversations between parishioners. Everyone seemed to be expressing some concern about the obvious and rapid deterioration of Father Carmeluchis' health during the past few months.

Paul stood around for ten minutes before stepping off the curb and hailing a cab that was headed north on Central Park West. As he entered the cab, Paul paused to read the sign on the door. "Twenty-five cents for the first tenth of a mile and twenty cents for each additional tenth of a mile."

He shook his head, smirked and entered the cab. "Northeast corner of seventy-second and third," he instructed the driver.

"Yes, sir.

Fifteen minutes later the cab reached its destination. Paul paid the driver, tipped him, exited and entered the corner cigar store.

"Good morning, Mr. Marshall. It's good to see you again. What will it be? I just got in some Royal Jamaicans yesterday. They are nice and fresh. I just finished smoking one myself. It was great!"

"That sounds fine, Ralph. I'll take a few to go." Paul handed the shopkeeper a crisp one hundred dollar bill. "Take out for the Times and Newsweek." Ralph nodded his head in acknowledgement and placed Paul's change on the counter.

After counting and pocketing his change, Paul bade the shopkeeper goodbye. He picked up his purchases, departed the store, turned left at the corner and headed to his house. Since it was Sunday, there wouldn't be anyone there. The servants were off until Monday morning. Paul had already decided that he would spend the day relaxing and reading. He wouldn't think about why he had really come to The Big Apple.

The first thing Paul did after entering the house was change into blue jeans, a red sweatshirt, with the initials USMC printed across the front in bright yellow letters, and a pair of white, canvas tennis shoes.

Ten minutes later, Paul was nestled into a plush, white, leather sofa in the living room, his legs outstretched, and his feet resting comfortably on the large, square, cocktail table directly in front of the sofa. He had already decided that he wasn't going to watch television, answer the door or telephone. Nothing was going to interfere with his plans to relax. It didn't take Paul long to slip into a totally relaxed state. He sat there for a long time, enjoying the peace and quiet. Eventually, he picked up the Times, sorted through it, and pulled out the business section.

It was exactly six p.m. when Paul tossed the last section of the newspaper onto the floor. He pulled himself up from the sofa, and made his way to the kitchen, where he prepared a light supper consisting of a tuna salad sandwich, a fresh garden salad and a glass of water. When he was through eating, Paul cleared the table and headed upstairs to the bedroom. The chimes from the magnificent, grandfather clock in the foyer rang out. It was eight o'clock. 'I guess I'll call it a night. I've got a busy week ahead,' Paul thought as he began to get ready for bed.

After a warm shower, Paul climbed into bed, propped a pillow against the headboard and leaned back. There was much to be done in the following week. He carefully traced the events of the past few weeks. Several meetings had taken place between him and the demon that first appeared to him the day after Mildred's funeral. During one of their talks, the demon explained how, in the execution of his duties, Father Carmeluchi caused a soul destined for hell to be snatched from the Devil at the very last moment and given to God. He went on to explain that when a person made a conscious choice to renounce his past life style, and vowed to live under the influence of the opposite force, that had been guiding them, that person's soul would belong to the god associated with that force. For having successfully performed the exorcism, Father Carmeluchi had to pay. The demon informed Paul that the time had arrived for the priest to pay his debt. Paul would merely help to insure that it was paid in full.

To aid him in his task, Paul was given one of the powers that the demon spoke of at their first meeting. At his disposal, Paul now had the power to cause Father Carmeluchi to experience hallucinations. His plan for carry out his first assignment had already been worked out in his head. He would attend the daily mass served by the good Right Reverend at Saint Aloysius. Paul decided that for the remainder of the week, he would give Father Carmeluchi a daily dose of his newly acquired power. Next Sunday, he would do what he had agreed to do. He would send The Right Reverend John Carmeluchis' soul straight to hell.

CHAPTER FOUR

It was exactly ten-fifty a.m. when Paul arrived at Saint Aloysius church. He walked briskly up the steps, and proceeded through the vestibule, as he had done the previous six mornings. However, today, there was one change in his routine. This time, he didn't bother to undergo the ritual Catholics normally went through upon first entering a church.

Once inside, Paul proceeded down the center aisle, genuflected and sat in the first row of pews. He purposely selected the same seat each time he attended mass that week. His choice provided him with a clear view of the altar. More importantly, it provided him with an unobstructed view of Father Carmeluchi, as he served mass.

Paul looked around the church. It was almost filled to capacity. The mass would begin in ten minutes. It was going to be a High Mass; all three altars would be in use simultaneously. Father Carmeluchi would be serving mass on the main altar. Two other parish priests would be holding services on the altars to the left and right. The congregation would be participating in the mass officiated by Father Carmeluchi. It was clear, that by time services started, there would be standing room only. A month earlier, it had been announced in the church bulletin, that this was going to be Father Carmeluchis' last mass at Saint Aloysius. His rapidly declining health led the Bishop to assign him to lighter duties at St. Patrick's Cathedral.

All three altars were ready for the service. Cloths of gold, colored silk were draped over the immaculately clean, pressed, white, linen cloths that covered the altars. The golden doors of the tabernacles reflected the numerous floral arrangements that decorated the altars. In the inner room of the sanctuary, several altar boys were conversing in whispered tones. In the outer room, the three priests were completing final arrangements for the triple service.

Father Carmeluchi was thoroughly engrossed in thought. The past week had not been a pleasant one for him. The trembling of his hands increased with each passing day. That wasn't the worse of it. He had begun hallucinating Monday, and experienced one or two delusions during each mass he served for the remainder of the week. He spent Friday afternoon and all evening Saturday in seclusion, praying to God. "Please let me find peace in death. Take my soul to join you in the everlasting happiness of Heaven. Dear God, I have served you well. If you are not ready for my soul, then please stop the trembling in my hands, and keep my mind intact, so that I may continue to serve you."

Father Carmeluchi thanked God for answering his prayers while he finished preparations for mass. He awoke that morning surprised and overjoyed, when he realized that his hands were no longer trembling. It was the first time they stopped shaking in a year. They were still steady hours later. He felt confident that The Lord had answered his prayers, and that he could serve mass, uninterrupted by trembling hands and images of things that were not there. After a final adjustment to his vestments, he informed the other priests that he was ready to begin the service.

A minute later, the preparations for mass were complete. The altar boys were all in line, and ready to begin the procession onto the altar. Father Carmeluchi picked up his chalice, took his place at the rear of the line, nodded his head and signaled for the procession to begin.

The opening blessing, the reading of the gospel, and the entire triple service until the consecration, where they were now at, had been in perfect synchronization. At the same time Father Carmeluchi began the consecration, the priests on each of the side altar were also preparing for Holy Communion. There was absolute silence throughout the church as Father Carmeluchi turned to the congregation. His outstretched arms were raised high above his head. He held a host firmly between his thumbs and index fingers as he proceeded with the consecration. The blessing of the host was the most important part of the entire ceremony. It was at this point in the mass that the unblessed host, once consecrated, became the symbolic body of Christ. Father Carmeluchi was reciting the accompanying words to the ceremony when suddenly he felt his hands began to tremble once again. He momentarily froze while looking up at the cross atop the altar and in a hushed tone pleaded. "Dear God, please not again. I beg of you."

As he prayed to God, his hands stopped shaking and were steadied again. He proceeded with the ritual. "Body of Christ…"

Before he could continue, his eyes fell on the raised host.

It was happening again, just as it had all week, at the same point in the mass. He looked at the host. He no longer saw it as a plain host. It now appeared to him as some type of viewing screen. He was taken back at what he was seeing. Images of the exorcist he had performed, and alternating images of the demon that had contacted Paul, was what he found himself staring at.

Father Carmeluchi closed his eyes, and began praying again in hushed tones. "Almighty Father, please hear my pleas. In Your goodness and kindness please let me finish this mass in peace."

Father Carmeluchi opened his eyes and looked at the host. Everything seemed back to normal. He proceeded with the mass. When he was almost done consecrating the hosts, the part of the ritual that signaled the completion of the consecration, and was in the process of breaking off a piece to place on his tongue a sharp pain radiated down his neck. He closed his eyes, shook his head and wrenched in pain. He froze momentarily in a trance-like state, afraid to reopen his eyes and continue with the mass.

After a few seconds of silence from Father Carmeluchi, members of the congregation began to raise their heads to see why the priest had stopped serving the mass. The abrupt noise from the fidgeting of the congregation brought Father Carmeluchi out of his trance. Again, he attempted to continue with the service. He tightened his thumb and index fingers on the host. When he tried to break it this time, the hallucinations began again. With a concentrated effort, he managed to break off a piece of the host. As it broke apart, the larger piece in his left hand began to cast off a light glow before changing its appearance. The piece he was holding no longer appeared to be a host. To him, it seemed to be a miniature person minus its head. The piece in his right hand now held the head of the imagined figure in his left.

Father Carmeluchi took a step back, simultaneously dropping the pieces of host, he had been clinging ever-so-tightly between his fingers. He immediately spun around toward the altar. Simultaneously with a sweeping motion of his hand, he shoved one of the two chalices on the altar sending it over the side crashing onto the floor.

The members of the startled congregation began to rise, dismayed by the sudden strange actions of their pastor. They seemed strange to all present, except Paul. Paul had succeeded at what he came to Saint Aloysius to accomplish. While Father Carmeluchi continued with his blasphemy of God, Paul sat poised, half kneeling and half seated, anxious to see what would happen next.

By now, the entire congregation was standing, and staring in horror as they listened to their pastor's ranting and raving. The two priests, who been serving masses on the side altars, stopped their services and headed toward the main altar. As they rounded the corner, there was a loud creaking sound above the altar. Both priests stopped, and tilted their heads in the direction of the sound. It seemed to have come from behind the huge crucifix that hung above the altar. Upon hearing nothing else, the priests again turned their attention to Father Carmeluchi who was now screaming curses at God. They were hurrying toward Father Carmeluchi to restrain him. They were only feet away from him when a thunderous sound echoed throughout the church.

For a brief moment, there was complete silence in the church. The looks of dismay on the faces of the worshipers quickly turned to looks of fear. The two priests ceased their forward movement and quickly rotated their heads, as though they expected to see where the sound came from.

Their visual search for the thunderous sound was brought to an abrupt halt by the screaming of several parishioners. The priests and the rest of the worshipers turned toward the screamers, momentarily forgetting about Father Carmeluchi. The now hysterical parishioners had a look of fright and utter shock across their faces as they stared in the direction of the altar. Both priests and the rest of the congregation turned their heads back around to see what the parishioners were screaming about.

Just as their eyes were settling on the huge crucifix, a loud crackling sound could be heard coming from behind the life-sized crucifix. The sound grew louder. Almost the entire congregation began screaming in horror. Their screaming instantaneously snapped Father Carmeluchi back into reality. He spun around facing the altar. The collective screams of the worshipers were so loud that Father Carmeluchi could not hear the other priests cry out a warning to him. "Look out!"

It was too late. Father Carmeluchi stood frozen, staring up at the crucifix, as it broke free from the restraining bolts, which held it in place, and tumbled downward, impacting him on the head. The force from the crucifix was so great that it broke his neck. He fell toward the altar in front of him. His forehead struck the jeweled, gold chalice still on the altar. It cut into his head. Blood immediately began gushing out. The impact of the falling crucifix killed Father Carmeluchi instantly. The force of the cross hitting him was so great that as he dropped to his knees and onto the floor, the chalice that had cut into his forehead remained embedded there. Panic overcame multiple members of the congregation. They began fleeing in panic toward the exit at the rear of church. Others stood motionlessly in the rows of pews; terrified by the sight of what they had witnessed just seconds earlier.

One of the priests, who had witnessed the tragic event, began shouting at the congregation. "Please remain calm." The other priest rushed to where the dead Father Carmeluchi lay. The crucifix had landed with the figure of Christ facing upwards. Father Carmeluchi's body had fallen partially sprawled atop the cross.

Several doctors in the congregation rushed forward to aid the fallen priest. The priest addressing the parishioners opened the gate and ushered them to the top of the altar. As they stepped onto the altar, the priest who had rushed to Father Carmeluchis' aid looked at the stunned parishioners. He paused for a moment before nodding his head and addressing them.

"There is nothing that we can do for him now. May the Lord have mercy on his soul."

The priest immediately began administering the sacrament of Last Rights to Father Carmeluchi. The other priest asked the congregation, which had begun to settle down, to please join him in praying for the repose of their dead pastor's soul.

When last rights were completed, Father Houk, the priest who had been leading the congregation in prayer, asked everyone to exit the church in a quiet and orderly manner. The frightened, horrified and the still stunned parishioners began to slowly file out of the church. Some weep openly, others fought back the tears as they left, occasionally turning their heads to get a last glance at the horrible scene on the altar.

Within minutes, everyone had exited the church except Paul. He was leaning back in the pew staring wide-eyed at the motionless body lying at foot of the altar. Paul was so preoccupied with his thoughts that he hadn't noticed Father Houk coming toward him until he felt the hand on his left shoulder. Startled by the hand that now rested firmly on his shoulder, Paul jumped to his feet. The priest addressed Paul in a hushed tone, "Sorry, sir, I will have to ask you to leave."

Paul nodded his head, signaling that he understood. He then slowly proceeded to exit the church. Halfway down the aisle, Paul turned around and looked back at the ghastly sight. Blood was dripping from the edge of the cloth covering the altar.

Immediately after Paul left the church, Father Houk locked the church doors, and headed back to the altar. The other priest had gone to call the authorities and the Bishop. When he reached the altar, Father Houk knelt at the foot of it, made the sign of the cross, and began praying again for the repose of the Right Reverend Carmeluchi's departed soul. He prayed for about five minutes. After he was done, he stood up slowly and covered his mouth. It was all that he could do to prevent himself from vomiting. It was indeed a ghastly sight to behold. He wasted no time in turning away. His eyes fell on Father Carmeluchi's missal at the top of the altar. Father Houk headed up the steps to retrieve the missal. He wanted to rest it in Father Carmeluchi's hands. Immediately upon reaching the top of the altar, Father Houk reached for the missal, but stopped when his fingers touched something. He yanked his hand away, stepped back and stared at the open missal. It was spotted with blood. He stood there for a few seconds before cautiously stepping forward. Using the greatest of care, he picked up the blood stained missal. He did not want to lose the last page that Father Carmeluchi had been reading from. Father Houk took a deep breath, then turned back to where the body of Father Carmeluchi lay. He began to read aloud from the prayer book.

"My cup runneth over with blood."

CHAPTER FIVE

July was Paul's favorite time of the year in Ramsey. The numerous hills surrounding his plush estate held the cool morning air captive for the better part of the day. Paul was seated comfortably next to the pool enjoying the early morning breeze before the stifling afternoon heat took over. The view from poolside was spectacular. Nestled in between the hills in the distance of his estate were countless variety of lush trees and fields of wild flowers that blanked the ground in a wide array of colors. He was reading one of several articles on the same topic from a variety of national, international news magazines and daily newspapers.

The articles were about a strange occurrence in a catholic church in New York City back in June. Both church and civil authorities had investigated the incident using every available resource. Six weeks later, the experts were still trying to find an acceptable explanation. There were even people who were now preaching that Father Carmeluchi's death, and the circumstances surrounding it were a sign from God. "Armageddon is at hand," became the cry of religious zealots as they paraded through the streets in massive numbers in countless cities across the nation. Similar demonstrations were occurring on a daily basis in numerous other countries.

By now, the entire incident had become somewhat amusing to Paul. He knew that in reality, it was a simple affair. It was nothing more then a case of an eye for an eye and a tooth for a tooth. Paul pushed aside the articles on the incident at Saint Aloysius church, picked up the most recent issue of his favorite weekly news magazine, and began to flip through the pages. 'If they only knew,' he thought while he read an article on American, Russian and Chinese arms reduction talks. Each side is talking peace, while continuing to build more powerful weapons. All for what? No more than one ideology trying to reign supreme over another. The wishes of a handful of men being shoved down the throats of the rest of the world. When will the leaders of nations realize that what works in one country, may be predestined to fail in another one? The end result of the collapse of the Soviet Union in the final analysis yielded very little in the way of word peace or an end to the threat of nuclear warfare. The United States and its closest allies quickly identified other nations to fill the role of Evil Empire vacated by the breakup of the U.S.S.R. One day, before it's too late, humankind might realize that we are all equal. Humankind would come to accept the undeniable fact that we all can from the same beginning, and all one day facing the same end.

Paul closed the magazine and placed it on the table next to him. He stood up, stretched his arms, took a deep breath and let out a long sigh. He shouted to the gardener standing near the fence, trimming the bushes. "Beautiful day isn't it, Carl?"

"Yes sir, Mr. Marshall. Lovely day!"

After a few minutes of chatting with the gardener, Paul

excused himself and went into the house. The household staff was hurriedly moving about. He entered through the kitchen, walked to the stove next to the counter, and poured himself a cup of coffee. He was leaning on the counter, sipping the freshly brewed coffee, when the head housekeeper entered the kitchen. "Good morning, Mr. Marshall.

"Good morning, Elizabeth. How are you this lovely day?"

"Just fine, sir. And you?"

"I couldn't be better."

"What would you like for breakfast this morning, sir?"

"I think I'll skip breakfast. Coffee will do just fine. I've got a lot of paper work to catch up on. I'll be in my study for the remainder of the morning. If I get any calls, take a message and tell them I'll return their call this afternoon." Paul refilled his cup and departed the kitchen.

Seated in his study behind a large, oval, antique desk, Paul began sorting through a scattered pile of newspaper articles. One of them had a picture of a young woman with a caption above the picture that read, "Sheila Carter, a twenty-five year old American woman is this years' Nobel Peace Prize winner." Paul read the accompanying story so often during the past few weeks that he practically had it memorized. According to the article, Sheila had originally been assigned to a small South American country as a member of the Peace Corps. She was an excellent nurse, and was loved by everyone in the rural villages where she lived and worked.

Unfortunately, while she was serving there, a revolution took place. Although most American citizens were evacuated when the fighting began, a few chose to remain. Sheila was one of the Americans who refused to leave the war torn country. She wanted to stay, and do what she could to relieve the suffering of the wounded civilians caught up in the war.

Without regard for her personal safety, Shelia traveled from village to village giving medical aid and comfort to the wounded and sick. She didn't pass judgment on either side involved in the conflict. When a civilian lay dying from wounds inflicted, she did all that she could to provide them with needed aid and comfort. Often, she would gently take the hands of the mortally wounded in hers and lead them in prayer. She begged the Lord to forgive their sins, and have mercy on their soul.

The revolution lasted a full year. Without once giving any thought to the jeopardy she was placing herself in, Sheila stayed until the war ended. After the war, Sheila returned to the United States. She settled in Washington, D.C., and began to lobby for massive aid for the war-ravaged country.

Paul returned the article to the pile on the desk and picked up another one. The heading read, "Nobel Prize Winner To Wed Senior Senator From Arizona." He dropped the piece of paper back in the pile; his mind retracing the background information he had on the couple. The demon had provided Paul with the additional information at a meeting they had earlier in the month.

Sheila met the Senator at a reception held in her honor, following the announcement that she had won the Nobel Prize for Peace. Senator John Bourne was some twenty odd years her senior. He was instantly smitten by her beauty, grace and charm. He pursued her relentlessly during the first few weeks following their initial meeting. He showered her daily with flowers and other expensive gifts. She was flattered by all the attention, and fascinated by the entire Washington scene.

Following a whirlwind romance, they were married. It was the event of the year. The list of those in attendance at their wedding read like a list of who's who in world power. Gathered together for the joyous occasion were power brokers from the political, corporate and social worlds from multiple countries.

In Washington, the expression, Power corrupts and absolute power corrupts absolutely was proven to be true almost on a daily basis. After only a year of the Washington scene, the once innocent and sweet Sheila had succumbed to many of the temptations that came with life in the Capitol. She had tasted the lifestyle that power and money bought.

Not too long after they were wed, the Senator began to experience major heath issues. As a result of his declining health, one of the things he had to curtail was his rounds on the D. C. party circuit. At first, Sheila stayed home evenings, playing the role of the devoted wife and part time caregiver to her spouse.

It wasn't long before being both wife and caretaker to her husband began to take its toll. She became almost unbearable to live with. Sheila began to feel cheated and trapped. She started taking it out on the Senator. She constantly complained about always being home and never having any fun or outside social life. To appease his wife, the Senator insisted that she represent him at local functions. It was no secret that he was in bad health. It only seemed appropriate that his wife attend affairs and parties to represent him.

As the months passed, Sheila spent more and more time away from home, often not returning until the early morning hours. Rumors began circulating around the Capitol. She was acquiring a well-deserved reputation as a wild and loose woman.

Eventually, the Senator's health improved enough that he was able to resume a full, work schedule. When his current term in office was up, four years after he married Shelia, he decided not to run for reelection. His decision was based on several factors. First, he decided that he had served the public long enough, and it was time to enjoy the fruits of his labor. He had amassed a large fortune through real estate and other deals back in his home state. He wanted to spend some of his accumulated wealth engaging in things that hopefully would once again bring him and his wife the joy and happiness they shared years earlier. His marriage was deteriorating, and he hoped that by leaving the Washington scene and its accompanying evils, he could save it.

Leaving Washington seemed to work miracles for the Senator, as he was still called out of respect by those who knew him. The seven years since his retirement from politics had been good to him. His health had improved tremendously. The birth of their son Timmy, six years earlier, seemed to breathe new life into him. He returned to his private law practice and continued to amass a fortune.

Timmy's birth seemed to have a settling effect on his wife as well. The first few years after her son's birth, Sheila revised her role of devoted wife and seemed to relish her new one of doting mother.

Sheila tried hard to convince herself that she was content living life as a homemaker and mother. However, the fire that had been lit in her while in Washington was still kindling deep inside. Soon after Timmy began school, she could no longer contain her desires for the fast life she had enjoyed back in Washington.

At first, Shelia tried to keep her infidelity a secret from the Senator, but she had become brazen during the past year. She began spending large amounts of money on frivolous things. It finally reached the point where the Senator could no longer look the other way and pretend that he was unaware of her activities. Finally, he could no longer tolerate her so-called indiscretions. He gave Sheila an ultimatum. He demanded that she straighten up her act, or he would file for a divorce, and sue for custody of Timmy.

Sheila loved Timmy with all her heart. If there was one stabilizing factor in her life, Timmy was it. No one would ever take him from her, not even his father with his powerful friends and well-placed connections. She didn't care if he left her without a cent. Taking Timmy from her was a different matter all together. She realized that her husband was not issuing idle threats. With his connections, and the countless favors owed him, Shelia knew that in a court battle for custody of their son, it wouldn't be much of a fight. The Senator would win hands down. He didn't hesitate in letting Sheila know that it would be a no win situation for her if they divorced.

For the first few months, after the Senator issued his ultimatum, Sheila managed to maintain a believable front by pretending to have turned over a new leaf. She had grown to hate her husband, and realized that if she didn't change her situation soon, she would grow to hate herself as well.

At first she felt helpless. It didn't take her long before she made a firm promise to herself. She would find a way out of her present dilemma; a way that would give her custody of Timothy.

A sudden knock on the door jolted Paul back to the present. "Yes, who is it?"

"It's me, Mr. Marshall."

"Come in, Elizabeth. What is it?"

"I have a Mr. Bourne on hold on the telephone. I told him that you were busy, and couldn't answer the phone right now. He insisted that I tell you he was on the line. What do you want me to tell him?"

"That's ok Elizabeth. I've been expecting his call. I'll take it. Thanks."

"You're welcome," the housekeeper responded as she exited the den.

As soon as the door closed, Paul leaned forward in his chair, picked up the phone receiver, and slowly raised it to his ear. "Senator Bourne, I'm glad that you could return my call so soon."

"When I arrived at the office this morning, my secretary told me that you called. She informed me that you said it was urgent. I returned your call as soon as she told me you called. It's not often these days that I get a call from so distinguished a businessman as yourself, Mr. Marshall. What can I do for you?

"Well, Senator....."

"Please, call me John."

"Only if you'll call me Paul."

"Agreed."

"I'll get straight to the point, John. Marshall Enterprises is ready to build another factory for our heavy machinery division. We've settled on Arizona as the ideal location, and are in the process of selecting and acquiring the land on which to build. I'm told that you're the right man to see for the best deal."

"I'm flattered that I'm thought of so highly on the East Coast. I sincerely hope that I can be of some assistance. When can we get together to discuss this matter further?"

"How about Thursday or Friday? I have to be in Phoenix Wednesday evening for a meeting."

"We could meet Thursday. Have you made plans after your meeting?"

"Nothing in particular."

"Good! What if I have my driver pick you up at your hotel Thursday morning, and bring you out to our house? My wife and I would be honored if you would stay the weekend. It would give you and I time to look over a few possible sites for your plant, and maybe iron out a deal."

"I don't want to impose on you."

"No imposition at all. My wife and I would love to have you as a guest in our home."

"If you insist. I'm registered at the Phoenix Country House. Are you familiar with it?"

"Of course. It's one of our finest hotels. What time would you like my driver to pick you up?"

"Eight would work for me. How does that suit you?"

"It suits me just fine. I'm looking forward to meeting you, Paul."

"And I'm looking forward to meeting you, John. I'll see you Thursday morning."

Paul hung up the receiver, leaned back in the chair, placed

his feet on the desktop and cracked a smile. Things were working out better then he expected. He did indeed eagerly anticipate meeting the ex-senator and his beautiful young wife.

CHAPTER SIX

The sudden and unexpected ringing of the telephone woke Paul from a deep, peaceful sleep. He reached atop the night table, fumbled for the telephone receiver, picked it up and placed it next to his ear as the operator greeted him. "Good morning, Sir. This is the wakeup call you requested"

"Thanks," Paul mumbled still half asleep. He hung up the receiver, let out a long, deep yawn as he climbed out of bed, stretched his long lean frame and slowly strolled into the bathroom. Thirty minutes later, he reemerged freshly showered and clean shaved.

He called for room service and ordered a light breakfast, consisting of two fried eggs, a slice of whole wheat toast and a glass of grapefruit juice. Minutes later, there was a knock on the door. Paul took his time walking to the door and opening it. He was cheerfully greeted by the bellhop. "Your breakfast, sir."

Paul stepped aside, and motioned for him to enter. The bellhop proceed into the room pushing the serving cart past Paul. He set the cart next to the table directly in front of a large picture window. After setting out breakfast he inquired, "Is everything satisfactory, sir? Will you be needing anything else sir?"

"Everything is fine. Thank you." Paul handed him a crisp ten dollar bill.

"Thank you very much sir," the bellhop responded enthusiastically as he exited the room.

Shortly after finishing his breakfast, Paul completed packing, called the desk, and asked them to send someone to his suite for his luggage. He looked at his watch. It was seven-fifty. His ride was scheduled to arrive in the next few minutes. Paul was anxious to meet the Senator and his wife; especially his wife.

After paying his bill, and checking out of the hotel, Paul was standing by the door next to his luggage, just inside the lobby, when he saw a black stretch limousine pull up to the curb. The driver got out and entered the hotel lobby.

"Mr. Marshall?"

"Yes," Paul replied.

'I'm Peter, Mr. Bourne's driver."

After shaking his extended hand, the driver picked up Paul's luggage and the two exited the hotel. Paul had already seated himself in the car by time the chauffeur placed the luggage in the trunk, and returned to open the door. The driver climbed behind the driver's seat, and pulled away from the curb. He had only driven a short distance when Paul addressed him.

"How long before we arrive?"

"Not very long, sir. We should be arriving in approximately fifteen minutes or so."

Paul spent the remainder of the drive lost deep in thought.

He had been looking forward to this day for weeks, and was more than anxious to try out his new powers. Beside providing him with the background information on the current status of his soon to be hosts' marriage; to further assist him in completing his mission, the demon bestowed upon him great charm and charisma. Added to his natural talents, Paul would have very little trouble winning Sheila's heart. Once she was sprung on him, he would offer her a solution to her problems.

Twelve minutes later, the driver was in front of the gate, to the Bourne's estate. He reached for the button on the dash that opened the security gate to the estate. and proceeded down the long, winding driveway leading to the main house. It was a large mansion surrounded by a sprawling, lush, deep, green lawn that highlighted the picturesque landscaping.

Moments later, the limo came to a complete stop in front of the steps leading to entrance of the house. Peter got out and opened the car door for Paul. "You can go right up, sir. I'll get your bags."

Paul slowly and deliberately strolled over to and climbed the steps of the Bourne's residence, pausing halfway to look around the sprawling grounds. The front lawn was perfectly manicured, and the surrounding bushes and trees were trimmed to absolute perfection. Paul smiled at the pleasing sight, before continuing his climb up the steps. When he reached the top, he rang the doorbell. Less than a minute later, the door swung open. He was greeted by a member of the household staff. "Welcome to the Bourne residence, Mr. Marshall. Please come in. The Senator and Mrs. Bourne are expecting you. They're in the sitting room. I'll take you to them."

"No need to do that." The servant turned around at the sound of his employer's unexpected voice.

"I'll show our guest in. See if Peter needs any help with Mr. Marshall's luggage." Yes, sir," Leroy replied, before excusing himself and heading down the steps. Both men took a few seconds to size each other up, then extended their hands formally greeting one another.

"Welcome to our home, Paul. It's an honor to have you as our guest"

"Thank you, Senator. I'm the one who feels honored to finally meet you."

"Please call me John," The senator quickly interjected.

"I've been an admirer of yours for years," Paul continued.

"Are you hungry, Paul? The former Senator inquired.

"No thanks. I ate before I left the hotel. I will have a cup of coffee, if it's no bother."

"No bother at all. There's a fresh pot on the table in the living room. Come, let me introduce you to my family."

Paul and John chatted as they walked down the long hall to the living room. When they entered the room, Sheila, who had been sitting on the sofa sipping coffee while playing with her young son Timmy, placed her cup on the table directly in front of her.

John and Paul strolled to where Sheila was seated. "Sheila, I would like you to meet Paul Marshall. Paul, This is my wife Sheila. Shelia, this is Paul whom I told you about.

Shelia extended her hand toward her guest. Paul reached out, gently took hold of her hand and greeted her.

"I'm pleased to meet you, Mrs. Bourne. It's not often

that I meet a Nobel Prize winner. To tell the truth, you're the first."

I'm pleased to have been met, Mr. Marshall. I'd feel much better if you would call me Sheila."

"That's fine with me Shelia, if you'll call me Paul."

"Sounds like a fair deal to me," she responded.

During their entire exchange of pleasantries, Paul and Sheila continued to look directly into each others eyes, barely pausing to blink. The Senator, had gone to the other side of the room to get a cigar from the humidifier on the mantel. He returned to where Paul and Sheila stood, and offered Paul a cigar.

"No thanks. Although I occasionally enjoy a good cigar, I'm trying to quit smoking all together." John turned away from Paul for a second. He had momentarily forgotten that his son was in the room, he quickly spoke again. "This is our son Timmy."

Timmy walked over to Paul and extended his hand. "I'm pleased to meet you, sir," Timmy said in turn.
"The pleasure is all mine," Paul responded while reaching for the youngsters hand.

Once the two finished shaking hands, Timmy's father told him to excuse himself because the adults had to discuss some business. Timmy walked over to his mother, kissed her on the cheek, bade his father and Paul a hearty goodbye, then skipped out the room. "He's quite a handsome little gentleman," Paul commented.

The ex-senator and his wife smiled and replied simultaneously. "Thank you."

"Please, have a seat Paul. Would you like that cup of coffee now?"

"That would be great." Paul responded while smiling politely.

"Shelia could you please be a dear and pour our guest a cup of coffee?" John grabbed the lighter from the table and lit his cigar. Sheila gave Paul a quick flirtatious stare as she addressed him in a sultry voice.

"How do you prefer your coffee?"

Paul immediately returned her look with a half-baked smile and responded.

"Strong and hot. No cream. No sugar.   Thank you."

As Paul and Shelia continued playing their little game, the Senator returned the lighter to the table, took a long draw on his cigar and held the smoke in for a good minute before slowly and methodically exhaling. As he continues blowing out the smoke, he took a few steps forward until he reached a reclining chair next to the sofa.

"I read about your wife's untimely passing a few months ago, Paul. While I realize it's a little late, I extend my sincerest, heartfelt condolences."

While the two continued conversing, Shelia slowly strolled back to where they sat and smiled at them. Her smile turned to a smirk as she handed the cup of coffee to Paul. While doing so, she slowly and deliberately slid her fingers down his hand. Her husband had unknowingly answered a question that was on her mind since first meeting Paul a few minutes earlier, "Was there a Mrs. Marshall?"

"Mind if I sit here?" she asked while pointing to the space on the sofa next to Paul.

"Not at all," He responded without a moment's hesitation while extending his hand in such a manner that her know that it was not only was it ok; it was welcomed. The trio spent the next several hours conversing and getting better acquainted.

Lunch was served around noon. After an enjoyable meal, Paul and John retired to the study, where they spent the next hour discussing business and perusing maps and photos of several possible sites for the proposed plant. They discussed the pros and cons of each before narrowing the list down to a few select sites. When they were done, John summoned his driver and instructed him to bring the car around front in fifteen minutes. He then called Sheila over the intercom. When she arrived, John was the first to speak.

"Paul and I are going out to look at a few properties. We should be back around six. Tell Carmen that we'll be dining at seven this evening. That will give Paul ample time to freshen up before dinner."

"Not a problem, dear," she replied while turning her head in Paul's direction. She smiled while continuing to speak. "I hope that the two of you don't plan on spending the entire weekend discussing business affairs. We have quite an exciting city. You should see a bit of it while you're here."

"She's right, Paul. Phoenix is a fun and interesting town. I have to fly to Dallas tomorrow afternoon for a few hours. While I'm gone, perhaps Sheila wouldn't mind showing you around."

Shelia didn't wait for Paul to respond. She gave him a quick, devious look and in a soft, somewhat sultry tone to her husband's suggestion responded. "It would be my pleasure."

"Good, then it's settled. I'll be gone most of the day. I should be home in time for supper. If my wife hasn't exhausted you with her sightseeing tour, we'll give you a taste of the Phoenix night life after supper."

"Sounds like a plan," Paul replied as he returned Sheila's smile.

"Give Timmy a hug for me," John requested of his wife before walking to the mantel, grabbing a couple of cigars, and placing them in his breast pocket.

"I'm ready when you are," Paul answered while momentarily staring intensely into Sheila's eyes. "It has been a pleasure meeting you, Sheila."

"The pleasure is mine," Shelia responded in a soft, hushed tone·

The two of them stood there half smiling at one another, trying to read each other's mind. They quickly stopped when John turned in their direction. He walked over to his wife and planted a kiss on the cheek.

"After you," he addressed Paul as he waved his arm in the direction of the door.

John and Paul spent the afternoon driving around the Phoenix area looking at various properties that might make a suitable location for the proposed new plant. Although he did a good job of feigning interest, Paul's mind was not fully concentrating on the business at hand. He was busy thinking of a way to extend his stay in Phoenix. He needed time to put his plans in action.

After viewing a half dozen different sites, and discussing the merits of each, they decided to call it a day. On the way home, they continued discussing the good and bad points of each site. Paul was only half listening. He finally figured out how he would stall for time around Shelia. When John got around to asking him which site he thought would best meet his needs, he would say that he was leaning toward the next to last one they toured.

"When we get back to your house, I'd like to call New York, and arrange for my vice-president of construction to fly down with a couple of company engineers and have them look the site over. If they agree on the feasibility of the site, we've got ourselves a deal."

"I'm sure they will agree with your choice. That site is a good choice," John responded.

They arrived back at the house half an hour later. Paul immediately placed his call to New York, then returned to the living room where the Bournes were seated, sipping cocktails.

"Well buddy, how did your call go,?" John inquired.

"There is a slight problem. My chief engineer is in Europe and won't be back until Wednesday. The earliest he could get here would be Thursday evening."

John responded quickly. "No problem at all. In fact, it's great. If you can, why not stay the week. I could show you a few more possible sites, and introduce you to a few of our prominent citizens."

"I don't want to wear out my welcome on my first visit. I'll check back into the hotel Monday and stay the week, John.

"Nonsense! I'll hear nothing of the sort. We insist that you stay right here." John looked at his wife as he spoke. She nodded her head approvingly. It was the response that Paul was hoping to get.

"Well, if you're sure I won't be interfering with any other plans you might have had.

"Not at all. It's settled then. Supper will be ready shortly. I'll have someone show you to your room, in case you want to freshen up," John responded as he exited the room into the hallway and summoned a servant.

Sheila strutted past Paul, brushing her body against his as she passed. When she reached the door, she turned, smiled, and in a somewhat seductive voice said, "I'll see you at super." As soon as she completed her sentence, she turned and departed the room.

A few moments later, John returned to the living room with one of the servants. "Leroy will show you to your room. I'll see you at dinner.

"Thank you. You're a most gracious host," Paul replied. 'Things are working out just fine' were his last thoughts as he exited the room and followed the servant upstairs.

Paul awoke early the next morning. He was awakened by the bight sunlight streaming through the skylight just above his head.

After rubbing the remnants of sleep from the corner of his eyes, he decided to remain in bed for a little while and ponder on what the day had in store for him. He also wanted to be sure that John had left for Dallas before he went downstairs.

After resting and thinking for another thirty minutes or so, he propped himself up in the bed, and began to retrace the events of the previous night. At first, he was thrown for a loop at how bold a woman Sheila was. Her constant flirting through out the day was easy enough for him to handle. However, at times, he found it extremely difficult to keep a straight face while talking with John during supper. Sheila had insisted that he sit in the chair closest to her. They had barely begun eating, when, shielded by the tablecloth; she slid her hand under the table and placed it on Pauls' lap. When her hand first made contact with him, he almost tipped over the glass of wine he had just finished sipping from. She slowly ran her hand up his thigh.

Paul coughed and covered his mouth with his hand, as Sheila slowly and methodically raked her nails down his thigh and back up again. His reaction to her teasing was immediate "Excuse me, I swallowed wrong," Paul quickly sputtered out, as he patted his chest with his other hand, while clearing his throat.

"Are you okay?" Shelia sarcastically ask Paul as she fought back a snug grin. Simultaneously she slowly slid her hand back down his thigh returning it to her lap. Paul fought to regain his composure. He couldn't help but wonder if John was oblivious when it came to his wife's' antics, or if he simply chose to look the other way. In any case, he didn't want to find out, at least not in a way that could be extremely embarrassing. Fortunately, Sheila decided to behave during the remainder of the meal.

Approximately thirty minutes after they finished eating, the three of them left for the night on the town John promised Paul the day before.

The drive into town was filled with idle chatter. At Sheila's suggestion, they wound up at an adult disco. They were seated at a table next to the dance floor. Immediately after ordering drinks, Sheila asked Paul if he would like to dance. Paul looked over at John for a reaction. "Please, be my guest, but I must warn you. She'll keep you on the dance floor for quite awhile."

John and Shelia danced continuously for the next half-hour. Occasionally, Paul glanced over at John, who seemed content, as he sat sipping a martini, and shaking his head to the beat of the music. They stopped dancing when the disc jockey slowed the pace of the music. As soon as they returned to the table, Sheila excused herself and went to the ladies room. Paul slid into his chair, picked up a napkin and wiped off the sweat that was dripping from his forehead.

"I warned you. She's some dancer. I used to enjoy dancing quite a bit myself.

When we first got married, you couldn't get me off the dance floor. Since my heart condition developed, I've had to curtail many things. It's been a long time since she's had a good dance partner. I hope you can keep up with her this evening. I haven't seen her enjoying herself so much for sometime now. Thanks for accommodating her."

"I should be the one thanking you. This is the first really good time I've had sense Mildred passed away."

Paul was indeed enjoying himself. It wasn't the dancing as much as the fact that things were progressing much better than he had expected.

It was two in the morning when they decided to call it a night. By the time they arrived home, Paul was completely exhausted. They had been conversing briefly in the foyer when John invited Paul to have a nightcap. "No thanks, I'm bushed. I think I'll call it a night," Paul hastily replied before heading upstairs.

CHAPTER SEVEN

By late Thursday evening, Paul and John had concluded their business. Paul headed back to New York the same afternoon. After dropping Paul at the airport, John went to his office in town to check on a few things. Meanwhile, Shelia was busy at home cooking a special diner for her husband. She sent Timmy to stay with his aunt for the week. She wanted to be able to concentrate fully on her diabolical plan for John.

John returned home early that evening. He immediately headed to the den to retrieve a box he hid in his attaché case several days earlier and tucked it in his jacket pocket. When the box was securely tucked in, John closed his attaché case and placed it next to the cabinet.

Shelia who had been watching him of on the monitor in the living room couldn't help but wonder what was in the box. She continued to watch as John tugged at the bottom of his jacket, straightening it out. Assured that the bulge from the box could not be seen, he headed toward the living room.

John wasn't sure if Sheila would be waiting for him there.

He just figured that the living room would be the most likely place she would be.

When he reached the living room entrance, John stopped momentarily in front of the large, oak doors to listen to the music coming from inside. The sound was distinctively Mozart. He stood for a full minute before he reached for the brass doorknobs. Sheila was still following John's every movement on the monitor. She watched him as he began to open the door. Sheila quickly reached for the remote and turned the monitor off. She then shook her head and threw her hair over her shoulders. She carefully crossed her legs, and stretched her arm across the back of the sofa.

As John entered the room, Sheila hesitated in her seductively posed position just long enough for him to get a good look at her. She stood up and sashayed over to him.

"How was your day dear?"

"Just fine," John replied, as he stretched his arms out for an embrace. Sheila delicately wrapped her arms around his waist and gave him a gentle squeeze in response to his firm embrace. She followed through with a quick peck on his lips before releasing her hold on his waist, and taking two steps back once again teasing him with a full view of her body.

"I've been looking forward to this evening all week," John uttered as he inserted his hand in his jacket pocket for the box he had placed there a few minutes earlier.

"So have I. I fixed your favorite supper. After we eat I'll draw you a hot, relaxing bath. Who knows, I might just climb in with you and scrub your back." A teasing smile crossed her face. John returned her smile and winked. He then pulled the box out of his jacket pocket.

"I have a little surprise for you. Close your eyes and turn around." Sheila closed her eyes and slowly turned her back to John. She felt her stomach tighten, knotting up again. 'I can't lose my nerve. I must go through with my plans,' were her thoughts as John's hands slowly encircled her neck. She felt something cold against her chest. The dress was cut low along the neckline in the front, accentuating her full, firm breasts. Her eyes were still closed as she reached to feel what had been placed against her skin.

As if he was giving a command, John instructed his wife to freeze. "Keep your eyes closed until I tell you it's okay to open them."

Next, he gently, yet firmly grasped her hands by the wrists placing them by her side, instructed her to keep them there and reached for the clasp of the necklace to make sure it was secure. After checking the clasp, he reached down and took Sheila's soft, delicate hands in his as he led her to a position in front of the mirror hanging on the far wall.

"Don't open your eyes yet."

He paused only long enough to once again gaze lustfully at the silky, smooth skin on her neck before leaning forward and giving her a quick kiss.

"You can open your eyes now dear," he instructed her.

Shelia was taken completely by surprise when she caught sight of the piece of jewelry that her husband had placed around her neck. Although she knew that he had hung a necklace or pendant around her neck, when her eyes first fell on it she was totally unprepared to see something so exquisite. The light from the recessed ceiling lamps bounced off the brilliant, flawless diamonds attached to a thick, shiny gold chain. There were eight two karat round diamonds in a V-shaped setting. A diamond that appeared to be at least four karats in size was set in the middle of the v-shaped ones. Sheila rubbed her hands over the diamonds, stroking them one by one. She lifted the face of the necklace away from her breasts. The prism of multiple colors emitting from the glittering gemstones momentarily mesmerized her.

"How do you like it?" Johns' voice snapped Sheila out of her temporary focus on the necklace.

"Like it? It's beautiful!"

"I wanted you to have it. I knew that it would look just as magnificent on you as I remember it looking on my mother."

His last few words were the last thing that she wanted or needed to hear. They cut into her like a sharp, surgical blade. He had to spoil the moment by again comparing her to his mother. It seemed that a day hadn't passed in the last few years that he didn't find something that she said, or did, that reminded him of his mother. 'Well, it doesn't matter,' Sheila thought. She hid her anger at his comment while forcing herself to give him a hug and a slight kiss.

"Thank you very much. I really don't know what to say except it's gorgeous."

"You needn't say anything. Your expression said it all," John replied as he smiled broadly with a look of accomplishment on his face

"Why don't you go into the dining room and relax.

Supper is ready, I'll bring it out," Shelia quickly chimed in, intentionally cutting John off before he could say anything else about his gift.

"Can I help you with anything my love?"

"No help needed. Everything is already prepared" was her quick response before going into the kitchen.

A few minutes later she returned to the dining room carrying a large, silver platter with a still steaming pot roast on it. "I'll be back in a jiffy with the rest. Why don't you pour us some wine while I'm gone."

"It looks delicious," John complemented her.

She turned and quickly returned to the kitchen. Once inside, she proceeded to remove a glass-serving dish from the cabinet adjacent to the stove and scooped some vegetables from the steamer on top of the stove into the dish she was holding. She was no longer feeling nervous. In a whisper she commented aloud to herself. "You didn't marry me. You married your mother. Well, enjoy this meal. I cooked it just like your mother used to make for you." That thought seemed to boost her courage for what she had in store for the great Senator John Bourne. She placed the spoon she had been using inside the dish of vegetables, placed a cover on it and returned to the dinning room. She set the dish on the table while smiling at John.

Shelia returned to the kitchen to fetch the remainder of "John's Last Supper." Two minutes later, she was back in the dining room, placing a tray of rolls and a bowl of rice in front of her husband. Hastily she walked to the far end of the dinning table and stood behind the chair in front of it. Without hesitating a moment, John got up from his seat, walked over to where his beloved wife stood, reached for the chair in front of her and pulled it out from under the table. Sheila slowly eased into the chair. As she sat, she carefully smoothed her dress beneath her, tracing the curves of her buttocks with her hands. After sliding the chair forward a bit, John returned to his seat at the head of the table.

Although she was seething inside, Shelia managed to maintain her composure through the entire meal. She was feeling nervous and extremely apprehensive, but she was determined not to let it show. She did an excellent job of hiding her true feelings. She spoke softly and teasingly as she told John of her after supper plans.

"I'll clear the table. You just relax. After I've put the dishes in the dishwasher and the food away, I'll be upstairs preparing you a little surprise. I promise that you will love what I have planned for you."

Shelia's thoughts contradicted her spoken words. If all went well with her plan, the meal, John just consumed would be his last supper. What awaited him upstairs would be his biggest and last surprise in life. She had no intention of sharing the bath she was about to prepare for him. She laughed cynically to herself.

It took her less than fifteen minutes to clear the table and tidy up the kitchen. After placing the last dish in the dishwasher, she turned the washer on and exited the kitchen. John sat in the dining room sipping a glass of wine. Sheila walked over to him, leaned over and kissed his forehead.

"I'm going upstairs to prepare the surprise I have for you. I'll call you when it's ready," she whispered in his ear before exiting the room and heading upstairs to their bedroom.

"Hurry dear. I can't wait to join you," John responded excitedly.

Immediately upon entering the bedroom, Shelia paused a moment as she went over her plan in her head. She looked around the room. She began slowly walking to the adjoining bathroom. Once inside she stopped in front of the large, sunken bathtub and stood there eyeing the empty tub, as though in a trance. After a few seconds, she reached for the button that activated the stopper with one hand while turning the water on with the other.

The water immediately shot out forcefully from the facet. She waited a bit before sliding her hand into the stream of gushing water to test the temperature. After a quick adjustment to the water temperature, Sheila picked up a bottle of bubble bath, uncorked it and poured a small amount of the liquid into the stream of flowing water. After recorking the bottle, she placed it back on the shelf. She stood there momentarily watching the bubbles form as the water filled the tub.

It was as if she was performing a ritual when she reached for the water faucet. The tub was almost filled to the brim as she turned the knob cutting off the flow of water. She headed back to the bedroom. A few minutes later, she returned to the bathroom carrying an electric cassette player with a long extension cord attached to the end. She set the cassette player down beside the tub, as she stared at the tub full of water with its hundreds of multi-colored bubbles. She stood there briefly before walking over to the wall opposite the tub, carefully stretching the attached cord as she went.

When she reached the wall she let the remainder of the chord drop to the floor. She returned to the tub and knelt in front of it on one knee. While exercising the greatest of caution she carefully picked the cassette player off the floor and placed it a couple of inches from the edge of the tub before pushing the on button. She stood and began following the trail the chord made to where she had dropped it earlier and firmly plugged it into the outlet. The tape began begin playing instantly.

She listened to the music flowing from it for a brief moment. The piece playing was one of John's favorite concertos. He absolutely enjoyed listening to Daphnis and Chloe Suite No.2. Suddenly, Shelia shook her head, turned away from the tub, and went back into the bedroom where she proceeded to strip off her dress and bra before he removing her heels and stockings.

Ever so slowly she strutted over and stood in front of the mirror on the closet door. She stood there with nothing on except a pair of tiny, white, G-string panties and a wry smile. She stood there for a few minutes pleased with what she saw. She was extremely proud of her firm, rounded, young breasts, her flat stomach, rounded bottom and long, sultry legs. She traced the outline of her body to reassure herself there was not a crease or an inch of fat anywhere on her smooth and soft skin. When she was done touching and admiring herself, she slowly slipped her panties off exposing her now fully naked body. She then inserted her two index fingers into her mouth wetting them. Once they were good and moist, she began rubbing her nipples until they stood erect and firm. "Beautiful," she whispered to her mirrored image. "I hope you enjoy you last look at all of this, John Bourne," she whispered before stepping away from the mirror, strolling every so slowly to the bed and climbing on it.

As she flung her head back, tossing her hair over her shoulders, she called out to her husband. "Your surprise is ready dear. You can come up now.

Seconds later, John who had been waiting anxiously appeared in the bedroom doorway. His eyes widened as he entered the room. The lust that emitted from them when they fell upon his naked wife stretched across the bed was crystal clear to Shelia. It added immensely to her sinister thoughts of what she had planned for him. He closed the door behind him and quickly headed to the bed.

Without hesitating a second, he climbed beside Sheila, and gently pressed his lips against her neck. Simultaneously, he placed his hands around her waist, slowly sliding them up along the curves of her body until he reached her breasts. He proceeded to gently take hold of a breast in each hand, and began to slowly caress them.

After a few moments of messaging her breasts, he pinched her now swollen nipples and began to gently squeeze them between his finger tips. Sheila shuddered as John released her nipples, and began tracing her body with his hands. He continued sliding his hands down her body until they rested on her thighs. He lingered there for a few moments until Shelia abruptly pushed him away.

"Patience my darling, lets take it slow. First, we'll take a nice bath together, and then we'll make love like never before," she teased him.

John remained speechless as he stared lustfully at Sheila's stunning, seemingly, perfect naked body. He was enjoying studying every inch of his wife's sleek, well-proportioned curves, her round breasts, the gentle curve of her stomach and her slender, tapered legs.

Shelia let him glaze at her a few minute longer before she kicked off her heels and slowly headed for the bathroom, pausing in front of the door before entering. John's eyes followed her every move.

Just before stepping fully into the bathroom, she made a three hundred and sixty degree turn so that he could see her in all of her glory. In a sultry voice, just like the one she used to teased Paul, instructed John. "Get undressed and join me."

As he was disrobing Shelia walked to the edge of the tub and checked the position of the tape player. 'When John climbed into the tub, she would allow him to lustfully look her over one final time and then kick the tape player into the tub electrocuting him. That would be the end of the almighty John Bourne. She could then begin her plan to seduce Paul and make him a part of her life. No one would ever suspect that it was any thing other than an unfortunate accident. Everything will work out just fine,' she reassured herself.

Shelia was so lost in her thoughts that she didn't hear John as he entered the bathroom. He proceeded to quietly tiptoe behind her, reached out and grasped her waist. His unexpected touch startled her. She whirled around as his hand made contact with her body, loosing her balance as she turned. John reached and grasped her by her waist. He struggled to hold onto her as he made a desperate attempt to catch her before she could fall into the tub. As he struggled to maintain his balance, his foot became entangled in the tape players' cord causing him to also loose his balance and his footing. The forward motion of Sheila's tumbling body pulled John forward with her, dragging both of them into the tub, pulling the tape player in with them. Sparks began flying everywhere.

The loud splash that their bodies made as they fell into the tub was almost drowned out by the eerie, loud, hissing, noise coming from the tape deck as it made contact with the bubble filled water in the tub electrocuting the couple instantly. The water continued to sizzle even after the circuit breaker shut the electricity off to the entire house. With the exception of the hissing sound still emitting from the steaming water surrounding the two charred bodies stuck to each other in the tub, not a sound could be heard throughout the entire house.

CHAPTER EIGHT

Paul was relaxing at home and reminiscing about the few days he spent with John and Shelia Bourne, especially Shelia. He was just finishing his first cup of morning coffee when his housekeeper entered the kitchen and with an extremely troubled expression on her face handed him the newspaper. He immediately pulled the paper from its plastic cover and unfolded it. There on page one in bold face print were the words: **FORMER U.S. SENATOR & WIFE FOUND ELECTROCUTED IN THEIR ARIZONA HOME.**

"So that's how you did it," he mumbled. Wanting to learn more about the blaring newspaper headline, he immediately turned on the television. He gave his undivided attention to the reporter as he listened to the account of the tragic incident being reported. He still found it extremely difficult to digest what he was hearing. He flipped from channel to channel hoping to hear that that it wasn't the Senator who was electrocuted in the tub with Shelia. He hadn't anticipated that he Senator would be sacrificed as part of the deal.

As reported, the housekeeper found the charred bodies of the Senator and his wife in the bathtub when she arrived for work the morning after the misfortunate and horrific accident occurred. Their deaths were being investigated as a possible murder, suicide or an unfortunate, tragic accident.

Paul folded and crumpled the newspaper before tossing it onto the floor. He picked up the remote control and aimed it at the television, changing stations. He was hoping to get more details.

A newscaster was just finishing up the story on the deaths of John and Sheila Bourne. The story was the same on every channel.

When she was through reporting the news about the Senator and his wife, the station went to a commercial break.

Halfway through the commercials, the word Bulletin flashed across the screen followed by appearance of another reporter who proceeded to identify himself.

"This is Paul Lang reporting to you from Washington, D.C. For the past several weeks, I've been providing you with updates as soon as they became available, relating to the news concerning the escalating developments in the worsening strain in relations between the U.S., Russia, China, and North Korea. This rapidly developing world crisis poses an ever-increasing threat to world peace.

I am standing in front of the White House, where a meeting between The President and the National Security Council has just ended. The Secretary of Defense, accompanied by what appear to be other high-ranking military officials are exiting the White House as I speak."

Without hesitating a second longer the reporter approached the Secretary of Defense, pointed his microphone at him and proceeded to try and solicit a comment from him.

"Mr. Secretary, can you share with the American people

what was discussed in the latest meeting?   We are getting reports that the ongoing international crisis has grown progressively worse during the past twenty-four hours."

Without slowing down the Secretary gave a quick and guarded answer. Several aides pushed the reporter out of the Secretary's path as he gave his brief answer to the question.

"Plans are being made to deal with the growing threat to world peace and stability," was his brief reply before entering his awaiting car.

"There you have it. The meeting had been cloaked in secrecy, as has the numerous other high level meetings that took pace here over the past several days. Back to you, Joan."

For an update on what has ben going on over the weekend we turn you over to Leslie Hall, our National News Correspondent, who has been at the Pentagon all day." A split screen appeared on the television showing the anchor and the reporter in front of the Pentagon.

"Good evening to you, Joan."

"Good evening to you, Leslie. What can you tell us about what is currently taking place?"

"Not a whole lot, Joan. Everything going on here is top secret. The Joint Chiefs of Staff had been in closed session all day."

"At this point, to your knowledge, has there been any information provided the press, or should I say the Nation, as to what was is being discussed in the meeting or any of the other meetings held there during the past several days?"

"Yes and no. Approximately fifteen minutes ago, a Pentagon spokesperson emerged from behind the closed doors of the War Room where this daylong meeting has been taking place. He held a brief press conference at which he informed us that all he could say for now, was that it was a strategy meeting being held in direct response to Soviet, Chinese and North Korean increasing hostility toward one another and threats directed at each other over the past several weeks. The Joint Chiefs are awaiting the arrival of the Secretary of Defense now."

As the reporter was speaking, several black official SUVs pulled up and momentarily stopping before turning right and heading down the steep ramp leading to the heavily guarded parking facility under the Pentagon.

"We have been informed that the Secretary of Defense has just arrived from the White House."

The split screen disappeared and the cameras focused in once again on the anchorwoman in the studio.

"For those of you who have been away trying to enjoy the weekend shielded from television, radio and newspapers, I'll recap the events of the past few days that have lead to these series of high level meetings. Three weeks ago, three unidentified, unarmed, missiles landed in a remote area of Northern Alaska. The Kremlin was quick to let it be known that they were not Russian missals. Their Ambassador flatly denied that they came from Russia. He went on to suggest that perhaps the United States Government should look at China, North Korea, or both, concerning the origin of the missiles. One of the two nations may have initiated the launching to force the United States to increase the amount of aid that the U.S. and other countries have been providing the two nations after a sudden economic and humanitarian crises brought on by a series of absolutely devastating earthquakes that struck both countries minutes apart weeks ago. The multiple quakes ranged in magnitude from eight point two to nine point two in both countries. Since the initial quakes struck there has been an almost relentless series of aftershocks ranging from a magnitude of five point one to six point two.

Fortunately, the warheads weren't armed and no physical damage resulted. The incident has become a major embarrassment for the Pentagon and the United States because the missiles penetrated U.S. airspace undetected by either our satellites or our first and second line radar defenses.

The Pentagon wasn't fully buying Russia's claim that they had nothing to do with the missals.

It didn't help matters any when, three days after the missal crisis, a recently launched United States satellite collided in space with what was alleged to be a Russian communications satellite. The Kremlin saw the collision as an indication that, although they denied having anything to do with the missals that landed on U.S. territory, the United States still blamed them. The White House and the Kremlin denounced each other over the incidents. Response to the second incident was swifts. The Kremlin announced that it was placing Russian military forces on an alert. As was to be expected, the United States responded in kind.

A series of high-level meetings, between diplomats from both the United States and Russia, that were being held in Washington and Moscow in an attempt to defuse mounting tensions were abruptly suspended.

Nuclear arms reduction talks, which had been taking place in Geneva for the past several months were also suspended and negotiators on both sides were ordered home.

The day prior to the satellite incident a series of events began to unfold along the border separating Russia and China. Friday morning, Russian sentries opened fire on a Chinese patrol they claimed crossed the boarder into Russia killing a Major, a Captain, and wounding a third Chinese officer and their driver.

The Chinese claimed that the attack on their patrol was unprovoked and that it was no more than a routine patrol, similar to the ones they conducted almost daily along their western border. They claimed they had not crossed over into Russian territory. Instead, they insisted that the Russian crossed the boarder into China and attacked the Chinese patrol.

The Russians claimed that the officer in charge of the Chinese patrol when requested to turn over photographic equipment, that was in their vehicle, refused to complying with the Russian request. Instead, the Chinese officer ordered his driver to turn around and drive off. The Russians made further claims that their sentries issued repeated warnings to the Chinese to stop their vehicle. They refused to heed the warning and attempted to proceed back across the border. Then and only then did the Russian troops open fire with their automatic weapons effectively halting the Chinese's attempt to escape.

The following day, a Chinese patrol deliberately crossed the border into Russia and seized twelve Russian soldiers guarding the border. The Russians demanded the immediate release of their personnel. The Kremlin accused the Chinese of committing what could be perceived as an act of war, while justifying their actions the previous day. They reasserted their claim that the Chinese patrol strayed into Russian territory and was taking pictures of a restricted area.

In response to the Chinese actions, the Russians have amassed multiple divisions of troops and massive amounts of military equipment along their border with China. The Chinese wasted no time following suit.

The Russian and Chinese actions have prompted NATO Command in Brussels to place all allied troops on full alert.

We have been told that injured Chinese soldiers are currently being treated for injuries they suffered and are being held at an undisclosed Russian military base in Eastern Russia. Their condition is not known at this time.

The Chinese government has been repeatedly calling for the immediate and unconditional release of their soldiers along with an apology.

As was to be expected, their demand was promptly turned down by Russian authorities.

Shortly, prior to a teleconference that was scheduled to take place between The President of the United States and the Soviet President, another incident occurred just inside the western Chinese border. Soviet pilots pursued and shot down, what they claimed were, two armed Chinese jet fighters. They alleged that the Chinese jets had flown more than one hundred miles into Russia. According to Russian news reports, the Chinese jets were shot down around fifteen miles short of their own borders while still over Russian air space.

As was expected, the Chinese denied having ever flown over Russian air space. They claimed that the Russians deliberately entered their airspace and shot down their fighters that were on routine patrol along the Chinese-

Russian border.

Immediately following the Russian attack on their aircraft, the Chinese military upgraded the state of emergency they had declared after the first incident. They placed their entire military on full alert, and began transferring additional large amounts of equipment, along with four more divisions of ground troops to their northern and western borders. The Russians responded in-kind. They also called on the members of the Warsaw Pact to back them immediately.

Since Saturday, on-going meetings have been taking place between Russian, U.S., Chinese and European leaders, in an attempt to defuse the ever-escalating crisis. No information on what progress, if any, has been make to defuse the biggest crisis facing the world since World War II. We've reported as much as we have been made privy to.

Please stay tuned to this station. We will provide you with any and all updated information as soon as it's made available to us. Now I'll return you to your local network. Good evening America."

Paul pressed the off button on the remote and the television screen blackened. He returned the remote control to the table, stretched his arms behind his neck, locked his fingers together and began to think aloud. 'The shit has finally begun to hit the fan. I don't care what anyone says, this isn't going to simply blow over. I just hope that the situation doesn't worsen before I complete my mission.'

CHAPTER NINE

Paul hadn't been visited by the demon for several weeks. He had been told that he would be contacted again shortly after he had completed his second mission. Paul glanced at the newspaper he had been reading and smiled. He had done what was expected of him and everything else seemed to have taken care of itself. He looked at the clock on the wall next to the bookcase to check the time. It was almost six p.m. A minute later there was a knock on the door. "Come in," Paul responded. The housekeeper entered the room.

"Supper is ready, Mr. Marshall."

"Thanks. I'll be there in a few minutes. You can take the rest of the day off. You can clean up in the morning."

"Thank you sir. I really appreciate it."

"Think nothing of it. You deserve it" Paul responded

The housekeeper turned and exited the room closing the door behind her. A few minutes later, Paul observed her on the monitor leaving the house and locking the door behind her. He lifted his feet, rested them on the ottoman in front of his chair, leaned back, and settled into a more comfortable position. In less than ten minutes he was fast asleep.

The sounds of the chimes from the clock woke Paul from a deep sleep. He promptly sat straight up in his chair and glanced at the clock once more. It was midnight. "I must have really been exhausted," Paul mumbled, as he stood up and stretched.

Just as he finished stretching, he heard a voice behind him. He was startled momentarily before quickly turning around. There in plain sight once again, in all his glorious might, stood the demon.

"You scared the daylight out of me," Paul shouted.

The demon paused, then let loose a loud eerie laugh. "Perhaps you would like to suggest a better manner in which I could announce my arrival." The demonic figure continued addressing Paul.

"You did an excellent job on your last mission. I knew that once Shelia fell for you, she would want to rid herself of her husband if she believed that she stood a chance of being with you."

"Why did you have to also to kill the Senator?"

"Chalk it up to collateral damage. All things happen for a reason. There are no guilty or innocent victims, just victims. Besides, the end results of these things are no concern of yours. All that you have to do is what I request of you, and I shall uphold my end of the bargain. There is one last assignment you need to complete, and then you'll have your wish. You will join your wife in her new home. The eternal kingdom of my master."

Paul flopped back into his easy chair before interrupting the demon.

"You're right. Besides, I couldn't give a good goddamn

about the particulars of this whole thing. My only concern is what my final assignment is all about."

"I was about to tell before you interrupted me." The demo responded to Paul with a broad smirk across his face.

Without hesitation, he provided Paul with details relating to his third and final mission. It involved a wealthy business executive. A self made multimillionaire. Who lived in Long Island, New York, and operated several highly successful businesses, with his partner. They had branches in both the United States and Europe. One rainy night several years earlier, when he was leaving his office, a young woman was struck by a car and thrown several feet into the air. She landed in the middle of the street, about twenty feet in front of where the car struck her.

The businessman rushed to where the victim of the accident had fallen and began rendering aid. It was too late. She had been killed instantly upon impact with the car. He saw a set of rosary beads hung around her neck and assumed that she was Catholic. He ran three blocks down Madison Avenue, and began pounding on the door of a church rectory. A secretary answered his banging. He hurriedly informed her of what had just happened. Accompanied by a priest, he hastily returned to the scene of the accident. The priest administered Last Rites to the victim of the hit and run.

A fire truck, an ambulance and several police cars arrived just as he and the priest returned to where the unfortunate victim lay. The paramedics examined the woman struck by the car and pronounced her dead. One of the officers on the scene looked in her purse in search of something that would identify her. He found a small wallet containing her driver's license.

A background check of the victim, by the police officer revealed that she had an arrest record that stretched a mile long. She had been arrested multiple times for various crimes. Her frequent encounters with law enforcement include criminal activities such as prostitution, pick pocketing, shoplifting, embezzlement and a variety of other petty offenses. Each time she was arrested, somehow she managed to avoid prosecution.

As far as the Devil was concerned, the priest who administered last rites, thereby absolving the unfortunate victim of the accident of all her past sins, had intervened in the order of things. The businessman who summoned the priest had to pay with his own soul for having robbed the Devil of the soul that was supposed to belong to him.

Once he had provided Paul with the information he needed to complete his final assignment, the demon disappeared without a trace; just as he had done after each of their previous meetings.

CHAPTER TEN

Paul spent the next few hours sitting in silence rehashing the events of the past few months. Finally, he stood up, walked to the mirror hanging on the wall, and took a long hard look at his image in the mirror. As he looked at his reflection in the mirror, in his opinion, he seemed to have aged quite a bit over the past few weeks. Paul turned away from the mirror, pressed on the remote light switch, turning off the lights and made his way through the darkened room into the hallway. It was now half past one. He knew what he had to do. Although he had slept for six hours already that evening, Paul felt exhausted. It took every bit of energy he could muster to climb the thirteen steps leading to his bedroom. Once inside, he didn't bother to undress. He simply kicked his shoes off and sprawled across the bed. In seconds he was sound asleep.

The early morning sun rays and light radiating from them shinned through the bedroom window warming Paul's face. The musical like sounds of chirping birds began to stir his sensibilities. He slowly opened his eyes, and was temporarily blinded by the brightness of the sunlight. He lay still for a moment, realizing that he had never undressed the night before. 'I must have been exhausted,' he thought as he slowly slid his feet over the side of the bed and stumbled toward the bathroom. His encounter with demon the previous night had exhausted him both physically and mentally. While he undressed, he reached into the shower stall, and turned on the water. He hoped that the brisk cool water would wake him and restore some of his depleted energy. He knew he had a long and busy day ahead of him.

As he stepped into the shower, he turned the faucets to full blast and adjusted the showerhead. The water splashed over his entire body. It was just the right temperature. Once he was thoroughly wet, he scrubbed himself down, rinsed off, and stepped out of the shower and reached for a large, blue, bath towel hanging on a marble, towel rack. He rapidly dried off, wrapped himself in a fresh, dry towel, opened the mirrored medicine cabinet and took out his shaving gear. He rubbed his hand across his cheeks and chin, examining the bristling stubble adorning it. After turning on the hot water in the sink, he wet his face and patted shaving cream across it with one hand. He held the razor under the flowing, hot water a few seconds before proceeding to shave the stubble from his cheeks and chin.

When he was through shaving, he opened a bottle of aftershave lotion, poured a small amount in the palm of his hands, and gently slapped the soothing liquid onto his now hairless face. He stared intensely into the mirror for a couple of seconds. He continued looking in the mirror at his now clean, shaven face. He no longer saw himself as having aged as rapidly as he thought he had when he studied his reflection in the mirror the night before. He was greatly relieved to see that. He stared in the mirror a few moments longer, still studying his reflection, before putting his shaving gear away, and returning to the bedroom to dress and pack a few things for his trip. The shower had invigorated him

Immediately upon entering the bedroom, he walk to the closet, removed two suits and placed them in a travel bag hanging on the closet door. He proceeded to his dresser and removed additional items. He packed enough clothes for a three-day trip.

When he was done packing, he made a phone call to a banker friend in New York City. It was eight a.m. Paul told his friend that he needed to see him as soon as possible. He let him know that he would be in the city by noon. They agreed to meet for lunch at one to discuss the reason for Paul's seemingly urgent call.

Paul hung up the phone and zipped his travel bag shut, removed it from the closet door, and finished dressing before heading downstairs.

When he entered the kitchen breakfast was waiting for him. He bade the housekeeper good morning, sat at the table, in the sunlit, breakfast nook and began eating.

After he was finished with breakfast, he called out to his chauffeur who was out front in the driveway busy cleaning the car. Paul turned to his housekeeper and informed her that he would be out of town for the next few days. A few minutes later, the chauffeur entered the kitchen and greeted Paul.

"Good morning, Mr. Marshall. Isn't it a lovely day?"

"Yes it is. I have to head to the city for a few days. I'll take the car and drive myself. Why don't you take the next couple of days off and catch up on some of that fishing you've been talking about a lot for the past few weeks."

"Thanks Mr. Marshall. I appreciate it very much. Here are the car keys. I filled the tank and checked all the fluids this morning. If you won't be needing me anymore, I'll be off to the lake."

"Enjoy yourself."

The chauffeur was out of the door in a flash. Paul turned to the housekeeper and told her that after she cleaned the kitchen, she also could take the next couple of days off.

'It was a beautiful day' was just one of Paul's many thoughts as he cruised down the Taconic State Parkway toward the city. The lush green foliage seemed as if it had been skillfully crafted, than painstakingly and methodically arranged in just the right places alongside the roadway. He glanced at the clock on the dashboard. It was nine-thirty five. He would arrive in the city in plenty of time for his meeting.

As he got closer to the City, Paul slowly went over some of information the demon had provided him with the previous night. David Jordan was an honest, self-made multi-millionaire. He worked extremely hard for everything he had accomplished in his life. He never took advantage of or crossed anyone on the way to the top. It seemed that he made only two mistakes in life, both unknown to him. His first was summoning the priest who performed last rites on the unfortunate, accident victim. His second, and biggest mistake in his life was trusting his partner too much.

Unbeknown to him, for years, his partner had been embezzling large sums of money from their various enterprises. Besides his thievery, David's partner had been carrying on a secret affair with his wife for the past five years.

'This assignment would be somewhat of an easy once.

He only needed to gained access to David's partners' and corporate bank statement for the past several years. His banker friend owed him several favors, and the purpose of the scheduled meeting was to call in one of them,' was just one of his thoughts. 'Getting David to believe that his partner had been embezzling large sums of money from their business wouldn't be difficult once he was shown the evidence,' was another one of the thoughts floating through his mind. The demon let Paul know that as usual, he needn't worry himself about the little details. He assured him that everything would fall in place.

The large clock in the center of the tool plaza read five past eleven. Paul flicked on the turn signal and veered into the exact change lane. The lines of cars trying to get across the Whitestone Bridge seemed to be moving at a snail's pace. That was to be expected during mid-morning in New York City. Paul reached over and turned the radio on as he inched his way toward the tollbooth. It took eleven minutes to travel the last quarter mile to the tollbooth entrance.

Once across the bridge, he continued along the Whitestone Expressway until he reached the turnoff to the Long Island Expressway west. Twenty minutes later, he found himself in a line of cars waiting to pay the toll to the Midtown tunnel.

It was just before noon when Paul entered the parking garage on East Fifty-second Street. He pulled into the valet parking area, stopped his vehicle and shut the engine off. Before climbing out of his car, Paul reached behind the passenger seat, and grabbed his attaché case. A young, Hispanic, parking attendant approached and inquired, "How long will you be sir?"

"About an hour and a half," Paul replied as he handed the

attendant the car keys and exited the garage. He had just about reached the exit when the screeching of car tires caused him to quickly turn his head. He barely caught sight of his car as it disappeared up the ramp leading to an upper level parking level. "Jerk!" Paul shouted as he speeded up his pace and continued to his scheduled rendezvous.

It had been some time since Paul had dined at Mickey's Place. When he entered the door, the owner, who happened to be standing near the entrance, recognized him and rushed to greet him.

"Well if it isn't Paul Marshall himself. Where have you been? It quite a while since you graced me with your presence."

"How are you Mickey? How's business?" Paul inquired politely of the restaurant owner.

"Business is fine. How are you?

"I am hanging in there. By the way, thanks for the flowers and card."

" I can't possibly express how saddened I was when I heard of Mildred's passing."

"Thanks. I am expecting someone in a few minutes. Do you have a table available where we won't be disturbed while we talk and enjoy some of your famous cuisine?"

Mickey waved his hand summoning the maître d.

"Seat Mr. Marshall at my table, and bring him a bottle of our finest wine, compliments of the house." Mickey instructed the maître d. who immediately reached atop the counter, picked up two menus and addressed Paul. "If you will be so kind as to follow me, Mr. Marshall, I'll show you to your table." Paul thanked Mickey, and followed the maître d' to a table in the rear of the restaurant.

Just as he was handed the menu and began looking it over, Paul was greeted by a familiar voice.

"Hi, Paul, long time no see. How are you?"

Paul stood up and greeted his expected guest. The two shook hands.

"I apologize for asking you to meet me on such short notice. Please, have a seat."

The two long time friends sat and continued exchanging pleasantries. They ordered a light lunch, and while they dined they engaged in general conversation. Over the years, they came to respect each other a great deal. Years ago, they had agreed, that during business lunches, they would never discuss business of any sort until they were through with their meal.

True to their long-standing tradition they enjoyed their meal while engaging in frivolous banter. Once they were through dinning and the waiter cleared the table, Paul refilled their glasses. They toasted their long friendship. After they tapped glasses and took a sip, Paul began addressing why he had requested the meeting.

"I suspect that you're anxious to know why I called and asked if we could get together on such short notice."

"That I am! Requesting a meeting on short notice is slightly out of character for you. What's up my friend?"

"I'm not going to beat around the bush. I'll get straight to the point. I need a favor. I need copies of some bank records relating to two of your clients. I can assure you that no one other than myself will ever know how I came by them. You know I wouldn't ask you for such a big favor if it weren't extremely important."

"You do realize what you are asking me to do?   Never mind. I'm sure you do. I certainly owe you enough favors."

"Trust me when I say that I would understand if you turn down my request."

"Whose records do you need?"

"David Jordan, Craig Peter and their corporation bank statements. Are you familiar with them?"

"Very much so. They are two of my biggest clients. I personally handle both their corporate and personal accounts. So what do you need?"

"All their business and person account statements for the past five years. I also need copies of all cancelled checks of five thousand dollars or more drawn on any of their business accounts for the same period. Can you get that for me?"

"Not a problem. I can get you what you want. Do you mind if I ask you what you need them for?"

"Trust me when I say you are better off not knowing."

"I can have them ready for you in a couple of days. Do you want to pick them up at my office, or do you want me to drop them off at your place on my way home?"

"I would appreciate it if you would drop them at the house," Paul responded as he stood, reached out and shook his friend's hand before asking their waiter for the check. The maître d walked over to the table and informed Paul that Mickey insisted on the house picking up the tab. He extended the owner's apologies for not stopping by to say goodbye in person, explaining that he had to rush out.

Paul thanked the maître d and tipped him a crisp fifty

dollar bill. The two long-time friends exited the restaurant and stood by the curb chatting. After around five minutes of conversing, Bob informed Paul that he had to make a two o'clock appointment. Paul thanked his friend again. They shook hands one more time, said goodbye and parted company.

CHAPTER ELEVEN

It had been several months since Paul last stayed at his East Seventy-second Street home. Like so much else in the last few months, Paul no longer had any feelings about being there. It had become no more than a place to hang his hat when he needed to be in the Manhattan. In his haste to leave Ramsey, he had forgotten to call ahead to let the housekeeper know to expect him, and to prepare the house for his arrival.

The first thing he did upon entering the house was open the drapes, allowing the bright, warm afternoon sunlight to illuminate the house. Next, he opened several windows allowing fresh air to flow into the stuffy house.

An hour had passed since he arrived at his townhouse. After changing into more comfortable clothes, he decided to take a walk around the neighborhood.

Paul spent the next fifty minutes strolling around before deciding to take in a movie. When the movie was over, he walked back home, got into his car parked out front and drove downtown to his favorite Spanish restaurant on Charles Street in the Village.

It was almost ten p.m. when he returned home. It had

been a long day. Tomorrow promised to be even longer. He reasoned that a nice, warm bath, and a good night's sleep was just what he needed. Without further delay, he turned off all the downstairs lights and headed upstairs to bed.

Paul work up earlier than usual the next morning, and spent the better part of the day sitting in his favorite chair while anxiously waiting for his friend to arrive that evening with the documents he requested. Since all he could do at the moment was wait for his friend's arrival, he shifted into a more comfortable position in his chair, closed the book he had been reading and rubbed his eyes. He glanced at his watch. It was two-thirty in the afternoon.

The day seemed to be dragging on forever. By midday. what had started out as a light drizzle that morning, had turned into a torrential downpour and showed no visible signs of letting up any time soon. He continued reading for a little longer before ever so slowly pushing himself up from the chair and tossing the book onto it. After stretching and letting out a long yawn he casually strolled to the window where he stood looking down on the streets below listening to the sounds the continuous downpour of the rain drops made as they landed against the windowpanes.

Paul continued peering at the street below and began to chuckle as he caught sight of a man who was getting drenched by the deluge of rain. The man was trying desperately to salvage his umbrella which had been turned insideout by an unexpected, exceptionally strong gust of wind. Paul continued to observe the man struggling with his umbrella. The victim of the weather condition continued to engage in a battle against the fierce, continuous gusts of wind while struggling to make it safely across the street. He was even more amused by the sight of three school-aged children running and playing on the sidewalk below. It was obvious that they were enjoying themselves. The rain and the wind seemed to contribute tremendously to the fun they were having.

Paul was still smiling as he walked away from the window to the bar, where he mixed his favorite drink. A few minutes later, he was mixing a second rum and coke. Just as he finished pouring the rum into his glass, he heard a knock on the door of the study. "Come in." The housekeeper entered and announced that a Mr. Bob Klein was here to see him. Paul cast a fleeting glance at his watch. It was five p.m. Much to his delight Bob had arrived earlier than he had been expected. Paul turned to the housekeeper standing in the doorway.

"Please, show him in." A few seconds, later Bob entered the study.

""Good afternoon, Paul. How do you like all this rain and wind we're having today?"

"Hi, Bob. It sure is a mess out there. I wasn't expecting you for another couple of hours. Come in. Can I pour you a drink?"

"No thanks, I can't stay long. I just got a phone call on the way here. I have to get back to the City to check on a small problem at one of our branch offices."

Bob reached out and handed Paul several envelopes containing the documents he requested. Paul grasped them firmly with both hands, and tucked them tightly to his chest. "Thanks, Bob, Thanks a lot. I owe you one."

"No need to thank me, Paul. It's the least I can do for

you. Well, I'd like to stay and chat awhile, but I have to run. I hope you find what you're looking for."

"I'm sure I will. Thanks again. I'll see you to the door."

"That won't be necessary. I can find my way out. I'm sure you're anxious to begin sorting through those papers. Why don't you give me a call before you leave town. It would be nice to get together for diner, have a couple of drinks and just relax for awhile."

"Sounds good. I'll call you when I can and we can set something up. Thanks again," Paul responded.

Once Bob departed, Paul proceeded to pour himself another drink. As he took a sip, he walked to over the large oak desk in far corner of the room, dropped the envelopes containing the bank papers on top of the desk, and seated himself comfortably in the high-back, black, leather chair behind the desk. He methodically untied the strings that held the envelopes shut, reached inside each envelope, and removed the groups of bank statements and several stacks of cancelled checks. 'Somewhere in these documents is what I need to start the ball rolling,' Paul thought as he began sorting through the checks and multiple bank statements.

An hour later, Paul was leaning back in his chair eyeing the piles of sorted checks and bank statements. Two of the piles contained checks made out to companies that were familiar to him. Several other piles contained cancelled checks that ranged in various amount from five to just under ten thousand dollars. They were made out to several different companies, none of which he had ever heard of. One by one, Paul carefully went over each check and made a list consisting of the dates, the names of the company the checks were payable to and the dollar amount of each check.

Next, he sorted through Craig Peterson's personal statements, and set aside the ones showing deposits that corresponded to the dates on the cancelled checks. After carefully examining each statements, Paul noticed that a clear pattern began to emerge. A red flag was raised. He painstakingly scrutinized the documents line by line. His suspicions were confirmed. He noticed that within a week of the drafting of checks in question drawn on their corporate account, Craig's personal statements showed deposits made to his account that matched the amount of the checks. There was now little doubt left in Paul's mind. He now had all the proof he needed to show that Craig Peterson had been stealing millions from his partner over the years.'

Paul wanted to confirm his suspicions before he drew a final conclusion concerning what he was seeing. He reached into his desk drawer, removed a large black telephone book, and flipped through the pages until he found the telephone number of a stockbroker friend who headed a firm on Wall Street. His call went straight to an answering machine. He left a message letting his acquaintance know what he needed and asked him to return his call as soon as possible.

The next three hours seemed to pass ever so slowly. The rain accompanied by strong, gusty winds was still falling at a heavy, unrelenting pace. What light there had been shinning earlier in the day was almost completely gone. The housekeeper had left for the day. Paul sat nestled on the sofa calmly awaiting a return call from his friend.

The constant downpour kept all except the bravest of souls indoors. Other than the steady, almost rhythmic beating the rain made as it beat against the house and the windowpanes, not another sound could be heard. The silence throughout the house created a somewhat serene atmosphere. Paul took advantage of the quiet and calm surrounding him. He reminisced about his past, and wonder what the immediate future had in store for him.

As with each previous assignment, the demon never divulged in advance to Paul exactly what his mission was and what would take place. Yet, the end results of his first two tasks yielded what the demon had wanted; two souls in return for the two souls that were stolen from his master.

He continued reminiscing. One of the things that he remembered, as if it were yesterday, was how he always enjoyed rainy days while growing up. He loved rainy weekends and always looked forward to them. As far as he was concerned there could never be too many or come too frequently. On those treasured days, he and his parents would spend the better part of the day together reading in the family room. A warm smile spread across his face. He continued thinking back about his father sitting tall in his favorite chair while slowly turning the pages of a book. His mother sat curled up on the sofa across the room from him reading a book of her own. He laughed to himself as he remembered how they teased him when he lay on the wooden floor in front of the fireplace, reading his favorite mystery novels. He could still hear his mother whispering to his father. "Look at that boy on the floor again. What does he have against sitting in a chair or on the sofa?"

His memories of his father looking up from the pages of his book and whispering to him, "It's easier to daydream while laying comfortably on the floor." Without saying another word, his father would return to his reading. As far back as he could remember the rain, coupled with the peacefulness and calm that always seemed to tag along with it, gave him a deep felt sense of inner peace and tranquility.

Paul was still sitting in his darkened study, listening to the continuous pitter-patter of the rain. He was reminiscing about his carefree youthful days. The sudden ringing of the telephone intruded on his solitude and thoughts of days gone by. He quickly bolted from the sofa, and darted across the room to answer the phone.

"Hi Paul. It's Sal returning your call from earlier. How are you?"

"I'm doing ok and you?," Paul answered.

"Can't complain. I had a tough time getting information on the companies you asked about. I had to cash in favors owed me by a couple of friends at the Secretary of State and the Controller's Offices. They just got back to me a little while ago. The companies you inquired about are all subsidiaries of the same parent company. A company by the name of Fidelity Enterprises, Inc. I had an even harder time getting information on Fidelity. I did manage to come up with something. The company is a Delaware based corporation. Heaven only knows what line of business they're in. It seems that the entire stock of the company is owned by one man, a Craig Peterson. That wouldn't be the same Craig Peterson who's partners with David Jordon of Euro-American, would it?"

Before Paul could answer the question, Sal cut him off. "Listen, Paul, would you mind telling me why you needed the information."

"Trust me when I say that you are better off not knowing. Thanks a lot for the information. I owe you one, Sal."

"You don't owe me a thing. I'm glad that I was able to provide you with the information you requested."

"Thanks for coming through, Sal. I knew I could count on you."

"Think nothing of it, Paul. Perhaps we can get together for lunch tomorrow? I haven't seen you in a while."

"I would really enjoy that, except I'm booked solid for the entire day tomorrow. Can I get a rain check?"

" Sure. I understand. Maybe the next time you're in town. I'm glad to have been of help. You take care of yourself."

"Sure will and thanks again." The two hung up.

Paul returned to his chair flopped into it and nodded his head as a smile of extreme satisfaction spread across his face from cheek to cheek. 'So that's how he did it. He filtered the money through a string of dummy corporations, right into his private account. Very clever,' were his first thoughts after his brief phone conversation. Paul continued to smile as he pondered his next move. He would make a couple of phone calls in the morning, followed by a quick trip to the post office, and Craig Peterson's elaborate scheme would be exposed before he could cover anything up. As always, he was curious how the scenario would play itself out once he had done his part. He had come to enjoy the anticipation that accompanied his waiting for everything to play itself out.

Paul remained behind his desk a few minutes longer before getting up and turning on the television. The news was on. Just as he had anticipated, the topic at the top of the broadcast was about the continued negotiations and numerous secret meetings begin held at the highest levels by and between multiple goverments around the world.

"For the moment, things seem to be at a standstill. No new incidents have taken place between the Russians and the United States, or between the Russians and the Chinese. The Russians are still demanding immediate and unconditional release of their personnel taken captive by the Chinese. The Chinese in turn, are standing firmly by their demands for an admission of wrong and an apology from the Russians for the downing of their aircraft. Meanwhile, the Chinese continue to voice outrage at the incident. They are stating that the action of Russia could be perceived as a deliberate and unprovoked act of war by the Russians."

Paul listened intently as the newscaster continued. "Although there have been no new developments between the superpowers to report on, the entire world is on edge. The concern here and abroad seems to centered on what measures the Chinese will take against the Russians, even if they admit guilt and issue a formal apology. A ranking member of the White House, who asked not to be identified, would only say, "We have been down this road before." He went on to express a widely held view by other world leaders that the Chinese were using the incident to distract their own people from the mounting crisis at home.

Before I leave you this evening, I ask that you join me in prayer in the hope that humankind will get through what can best be described as the darkest hours the world has seen since the outbreak of World War II. Good night America and all our viewers around the world." With those words, the newscaster signed off and the station switched to a commercial break.

Paul returned to his desk and began carefully separating the documents he needed to take with him to the post office in the morning from the others. When he was done with the task at hand, he decided there was nothing else he could for now except head upstairs and call it a night.

CHAPTER TWELVE

The weather Thursday morning was in staunch contrast to the stormy weather the previous day. The sun was shining and not a cloud could be seen anywhere in the brightly lit, blue sky. There was a slow, light breeze giving the air that all familiar crisp feeling that was characteristic of fall mornings in New York City.

Paul emerged from the bathroom, unwrapped a bath towel from around his waist, and rubbed his hair briskly with the towel for a few minutes. When he was done, he threw the towel onto the chair in the corner of the room, and glided his hands through his hair to confirm it was completely dry. It didn't take him long to get dressed. Once fully garbed he strolled over to the window facing Second Avenue, opened it slightly, and stared down at the almost empty street below. He looked at his watch. It was seven-forty and hardly a soul was on the street yet. He always found it somewhat amusing when he looked down at the almost deserted streets of Manhattan in the early morning. It always tickled him how the streets went from being almost void of pedestrians one moment, and then, presto, like magic, at a few minutes before eight, people were everywhere.

Usually, Paul would have stood by the window and waited for the throngs of hearty New Yorkers to appear, but there was work to be done. He opened the window and slowly took in a long, deep breath of the clean, early morning air, before shutting the window. He looked around the room and was momentarily saddened, when his eyes chanced upon a picture of Mildred perched atop the chest of drawers. He fought back a tear and began to speak to the picture. "It won't be long dear before we're together again." Staring at the picture added to the constant pain that he felt deep inside since Mildred's death. He forced himself to turn his eyes away from his wife's photograph and took another look around the room before heading downstairs. The housekeeper greeted him at the bottom of the steps. "Good Morning Mr. Marshall. I hope you had a pleasant night's rest?"

"Good morning, Mary. I slept quite well, thank you. You're here bright and early this morning."

"I woke up earlier than usual and thought I'd get an early start on the day. I was hoping that I could take an extended lunch and enjoy a little of this beautiful day. That is, if it's all right with you, sir?"

"Sure. In fact, I'll be gone all afternoon, and a good part of the evening, so when you finish tiding up, you can take the rest of the day off."

"Thank you Mr. Marshall. Would you like me to prepare supper for you before I leave?"

"That won't be necessary Mary, I'll be dining out this evening."

"Would you like anything special for breakfast this

morning?"

"No thanks. I'll skip breakfast. I'll just have a cup of coffee. I'll be in the study."

"Right away, Mr. Marshall. I started a fresh pot a few minutes ago. It should be ready any time now. I'll bring it to you as soon as it's ready"

"Thanks, Mary." Paul headed for the study, as the maid headed to the kitchen to fetch the coffee.

Five minutes later, Paul was seated in the study, rubbing his hands along the sides of a fresh mug of hot coffee. The room was a bit cool. The warmth from the steaming mug of coffee felt good to the touch.

"Ah, there is nothing as comforting and enjoyable than the first mug of coffee in the morning," he whispered. Whenever Paul was at home, he insisted that his coffee be served in a mug. "You can't caress an ordinary coffee cup like you can a mug," he continued as he slowly raised the mug to his mouth and took another sip. He paused with the mug still touching his lips, just long enough to take in the pleasing aroma of the freshly brewed coffee.

A couple of sips later, Paul put the mug down. He picked up the bank papers he intended to mail, put them in a large envelope, licked the flap and pressed against the envelope sealing it tightly. Next, he reached for the telephone directory on the bookshelf behind the desk, and flipped through the pages.

"Here we are, Euro-American Import and Export Company, Inc.," he mumbled aloud, as he reached for a pencil and jotted down the number on a small, yellow pad stuck to the desk next to the telephone. After scribbling the number down, he checked the number again to insure that he had copied it correctly, shut the directory, and returned it to the shelf. He yanked the piece of paper he wrote the number on from the pad, and stuck it on the envelope to be mailed. 'Wonderful little convenience,' was his thought as he patted the small piece of paper making sure it was stuck firmly to the envelope. He picked up his mug again, leaned back in his chair and placed both feet on top of the desk. He took a momentary pause from sipping his still hot coffee long enough to look at the clock on the wall. 'Only eight ten, I'll wait until nine before I call,' he told himself.

Paul knew that Euro-American Import and Export Company was a huge multinational corporation. He planned to call the main office listed in New York City to find out where David Jordon was going to be on Friday. He wanted to be sure that David received the mail he was planning to send without delay.

'It is indeed going to be a long and busy day. After I drop this little package off at the post office, I need to catch up with Larry,' Paul thought, as he swallowed the last sip of coffee and glanced up at the clock again. It was now half past eight. He spoke aloud to himself again, which is something that he often did in the solitude of his home. "I'd better give Larry a call at home. He's one busy attorney."

Paul reached for the telephone pulling it closer. He squinted his left eye, causing his forehead to wrinkle, as he took a moment to recall his attorney's phone number. "Six, six, two, one, four, two, four. That's it." He pushed the corresponding buttons on the telephone, and listened to the chimes as they sent electrical impulses surging through the line. He counted the rings out loud. "One, two, three....

Damn! I hope he hasn't left yet. There's no telling when I'll catch up with him if I don't catch him now."

Before he could finish his sentence the sound of someone picking up the receiver on the other end could be heard.

"Hello, Larry Andersons' residence."

Paul recognized his attorney's voice right away. "Hi Larry. This is Paul, Paul Marshall."

"How are you, Paul? I can't help but get nervous when I hear from one of my most important clients so early in the morning. I haven't heard from you since Mildred's funeral. Is everything okay?"

"Everything's fine. I had to come into town unexpectedly Tuesday and while I'm here I need to see you about a few important matters. I realize that you're busy, but I would appreciate it if you could squeeze me into your schedule today."

"I'm never too busy to see you, Paul. I'll be in court all morning. I'm free this afternoon. How does one-thirty work for you?"

"That's fine with me. Thanks. I really appreciate you meeting with me on such short notice."

"Don't mention it. I'll see you then."

Paul hung up and reflected on the past several months. He had lost interest in almost everything that had been an intricate part of his life prior to the passing of his beloved wife. Almost immediately after Mildred's death, he began delegating almost all of the day-to-day functions relating to the running of his corporation to various key managers. Four weeks earlier he had temporarily removed himself as President and Chief Executive Officer of Marshall Enterprises, Inc.

He appointed Harvey Stevens, his Chief Financial Officer and First Vice President as acting CEO. He told everyone that he needed to take a long vacation and think some things over. In reality, he no longer cared about the business and had no intention of returning to it.

Paul had become obsessed with the role he had taken on as an advocate of the Devil. As the principal stockholder of one of the world's largest privately held corporations, Paul experienced a tremendous amount of power throughout his entire adult life. Yet, all the power he had experienced in the corporate world could not measure up to the feeling of power he came to know while carrying out the tasks given him by the demon.

Abandoning his reflections, Paul brought his train of thought in line with the present. He decided to jot down a few of the things he wanted to go over with his lawyer. He reached in the top drawer of the desk and pulled out a pad of paper. He then reached in the crystal cup he used as a penholder and removed a sleek, white pen that use to belong to his father. He took hold of the pen firmly in his left hand, while slowly rotated the bottom half of it with his right hand until the tip of the filter was sticking out. As he angled the paper, turning the pad sharply to the right, he once again thought back to his childhood days. He remembered vividly how when he first began to learn to write, his mother would try to force him to use his right hand. He was a southpaw by birth. Out of spite, the more his mother tried to force him to use his right hand, the more he resisted. He remembered the big fight that his parents got into when his father found out that his mother had been trying to force him to use his right hand.

When he started school his first grade teacher, a nun at the parochial school he attended, also tried to turn him into a righty. He was the only southpaw in the class, and was often ridiculed by his fellow classmates. His teacher would do things such as seat him with his desk pressed tightly against the left classroom wall, thereby making it difficult for him to use his left hand. He was afraid to tell his parents about his teachers' actions. He knew that while his mother would condone them; his father wouldn't. He would go to school and severely chastise the teacher for trying to make his son into a righty. Paul held his ground, and resisted his teachers' attempts to turn him into a righty. Finally, midway through the school year, his teacher abandoned her efforts. He attributed the many attempts by his mother and his teacher to turn him into a righty, and his stubborn refusal to comply, as the one of the reasons for his business success. He learned early on in life that if you stood your ground, that perseverance would win out in the end.

Paul sat lost in his inner thoughts until the ringing of the chimes from the grandfather clock, in the far corner of the room, interrupted them. It was nine o'clock. He had lost track of time. He reached for the small piece of paper on the envelope with Euro-American's number written on it and quickly dialed it. For a brief moment, he was feeling a bit anxious as he waited for someone to pick up the receiver at the other end of the line.

After what seemed like an eternity, he heard a click. "Good morning, Euro-American Imports and Exports. May I help you?"

"Good Morning. This is Paul Marshall," Paul responded. "I'm trying to reach Mr. Jordon."

"Mr. Jordon can be reached at our San Diego office for the next couple of days. The number is, area code seven one four, seven eight five, one nine two three."

"Could you also give me the address? I need to send him some time sensitive and extremely important papers for him to go over."

"Certainly. It's 4510 Burlington Way, San Diego, California nine two one two six."

"Thanks."

"You're welcome sir. Have a nice day."

"You too." Paul quickly hung up the phone. He carefully copied the address onto the envelope containing the documents. He unfolded the paper that he had been making notes on, carefully checked the address on the envelope again before inserting the documents in the envelope. Reassured that the address was correct, he dropped the envelope in his briefcase and shut it. On his way out of the study, he paused just long enough to grab a jacket hanging on a hook by the door. He stopped by the kitchen to informed Mary that he was leaving for the day. "I'm on my way Mary. You enjoy your afternoon off."

"Yes sir, Mr. Marshall. I sure will. Thank you."

Two minutes later, Paul was standing on the sidewalk in front of his house. By now, the city was alive. People were hurriedly scurrying about in all directions. Several couriers on bikes could be seen skillfully weaving their way in and out of traffic. There was the usual gridlock at the intersections, and the accompanying beeping of horns from frustrated and impatient drivers.

"Good old New York," Paul mumbled. "Everyone seems

to be in a rush to get somewhere in a hurry."

Paul glanced at the deep, blue, brightly lit sky. A slight breeze could be felt as it flowed between the mazes of concrete towers that made up much of New York City. He continued staring at the sky a short while longer. He was enjoying the cool, refreshing, early, morning breeze he felt all around him. He decided that it was such a lovely day, that he would leave his car home and walk to the main post office on Seventh Avenue and Thirty-third Street.

It took Paul fifty minutes to cover the approximately two-mile walk to the Post Office. When he arrived at his destination, he hesitated briefly before climbing the seemingly, endless rows of steps leading to the entrance. After taking in a deep breath and exhaling it slowly, he proceeded up the steps. Half way to the top of the landing, he paused while taking in another deep breath, before climbing the remaining steps and entering the post office.

Once inside, Paul was glad to see that the customer service line was much shorter than he expected it would be at that time of the day. He proceeded to take his place in line behind four other people. Less than five minutes later, it was his turn to be waited on.

"Good morning. How may I help you?" was the greeting from the somewhat, jovial, postal clerk behind the counter. Paul opened his attaché case and pulled out the envelope he intended to mail. "I'd like to send this express mail, return receipt."

"No problem." The clerk replied while reaching for an express mail label. He handed Paul the label and asked him to step to the side while he filled it out and return to the counter when it was completed.

Three minutes later, Paul was back at the counter handing the completed label back to the clerk along with the envelope containing the bank papers. The clerk took the envelope along with the completed mailing label, inserted the envelope he was handed inside of an express mail envelope, and pasted the label onto the envelope. He flipped the mailer over removed the strip covering the glue on the flap on the back of it and sealed the envelope. "Will that be all this morning sir?"

"Yes. Thanks," Paul answered.

"That will be ten dollars and seventy-five cents." Paul reached into his pocket, pulled out a twenty-dollar bill, and handed it to the clerk. The clerk rang up the sale, inserted the money in his cash drawer, placed Paul's change along with a receipt on the counter and thanked him. Paul picked up the receipt along with his change, and exited the post office.

Once outside, he stood on the top step of the landing, and looked around at the hundreds of people hurrying to and from Penn Station. He repeatedly glanced up and down Fashion Avenue at the thousands of people hurrying about while taking extreme care not get run over by the numerous racks of garments being pushed up and down the street and adjacent sidewalks. It amazed him how everyone seemed oblivious to the crisis that was unfolding on the other side of the world. 'It's as if nothing is going on anywhere except right here,' Paul thought as he descended the steps, walked over to the newsstand on the corner and purchased the New York Times. He looked at the headline, "THE WORLD HOLDS ITS' BREATH AS Russia AND CHINA STAND BY THEIR DEMANDS."

The entire front page was devoted to various accounts about the mounting world crisis. Paul rolled the paper up and tucked it under his arm. He took another look at the thousands of people moving about in all directions while turning his head from left to right. Not a soul in his view seemed to care about anything other than the moment they were in. He envisioned what was probably going on in Ramsey and thousands of small cities, villages and towns around the world. Everyone in those places was probably talking about nothing else except the deepening world crisis. He reasoned that hundreds of millions of people around the world were busy contemplating what would happen should the worse case scenario unfold. 'Maybe New Yorkers have the right idea. There won't be a damn thing anyone could do to save him or herself if negotiations did not resolve the crisis. Good old New Yorkers; the only true, optimistic, realists left in the world.'

His train of thought was broken when a shabbily dressed man, who appeared to be in his late twenties, approached him and respectfully asked if he could spare any change. Paul reached in his pocket pulled out a crisp twenty-dollar bill and handed it to the man who was apparently down on his luck. The panhandler could not believe the stranger's generosity when he unfolded the bill Paul had given him. He looked around before quickly tucking the bill deep inside the pocket of his tattered trousers. He thanked Paul profusely for his generosity before turning away and heading in the opposite direction.

Paul glanced at his watch. It was only ten-fifty. His appointment with Larry wasn't for another two hours and fifteen minutes. He stood there for a few moments while he thought about what he could do to kill some time. He decided to drop by his company headquarters to see how things were going. Most of the employees at Marshall Enterprises' central office had been with Paul a long time. He considered them more than just employees. Over the years he had come to view many of them as friends and extended family. One of the reasons he wanted to see his attorney had to do with them.

Paul stepped off the curb and hailed a taxi. As soon as the cab driver pulled over, he rushed over and entered it before someone else beat him to the cab. He climbed into the rear seat, leaned forward, and spoke through the multiple rows of holes in the protective glass that separated him from the drive.

"Number Two World Trade Center." The driver scribbled the address onto his trip log, pulled away from the curb and headed downtown.

When he arrived at his corporate headquarters everyone was both surprised and extremely glad to see him. He spent the next hour engaging in conversations with various employees before saying goodbye and heading home.

CHAPTER THIRTEEN

David Jordon sat upright in his seat, alternating between staring blankly out of the window at the clouds below, and the pile of documents on the tray in front of him. He felt anger, hurt and betrayal. He wasn't sure which of the three feelings he was experiencing was the strongest. 'There is an explanation. Craig can explain everything. Who am I kidding? It's all right here in front of me. He's been stealing me blind for God only knows how long. Why? We were like brothers. Hell, if I can't trust Craig, who else can I trust, except Sandy,' were a few of the thoughts racing through his mind.

David and Sandy had recently celebrated their twenty-first wedding anniversary. They were high school sweethearts, and married shortly after graduation. He and Craig had been friends since the second grade. They attended the same schools all the way through high school. They spent countless hours, while growing up, making future plans. Less than a year after high school graduation, they were business partners. They started by buying knickknacks and other odds and ends wholesale. They then resold the merchandise to stores and at various flea markets around town, and out on

Long Island. Within two years, they were selling wholesale in bulk to other aspiring entrepreneurs and local businesses. Over the course of several years, they expanded their business at a steady but measured pace. In twenty years, they built what had started out as basically a flea market operation into the Euro-American Import and Export Company, Inc. Their company was now one of the largest companies of its kind in the United States.

David continued to ponder. 'Why, would Craig steal from me?' They had made millions over the years and were now paying themselves in excess of two million dollars a year each in salary and bonuses. Additional compensation by way of benefits such as company cars, unlimited first class travel, and dining at the finest restaurants around the world were just a few of the other lavish perks they bestowed on themselves. It made no sense.' A flight attendant interrupted David's thoughts.

"Excuse me, sir, can I get you another drink or anything else?"

He had been so deep into his thoughts that that the flight attendant's voice startled him. David popped his head up.

"Another drink would be fine. Thank you." He gathered the papers from the tray in front of him, stuffed them back into their envelope, and placed it on the empty seat next to him. The flight attendant returned a few minutes later with his drink.

"Here you are sir, one bottle of scotch and a side of soda." She leaned forward and placed the small bottle of scotch along with a glass of ice and soda on the tray in front of him.

"Thank you very much."

"You're quite welcome. Can I get you anything else?"

"No thank you. This is fine."

"Well if you change your mind, don't hesitate to ask." The flight attendant smiled, and returned to her station at the front of the plane.

David opened the bottle of scotch, and poured it into the glass containing the ice and soda. He shook the glass slightly, mixing the drink, and began slowly sipping it. He returned to his previous train of thoughts. 'It's bad enough with the world crisis nearly causing our supplies to be cut off. I've got tons of goods sitting in storage hangers at various airports and at the docks, on both coasts, waiting to be shipped and there isn't a damn thing we can do about it. If that wasn't bad enough, just yesterday his insurance company notified him that in thirty days they would no longer be underwriting import/export insurance policies because of the risk involved based on the current state of globally affairs.' He gulped the remainder of his drink down in one swallow, then leaned out into the isle, and signaled the flight attendant. Moments later, the attendant strolled over to David's seat.

"Can I get you something else?"

"I'll have another," David replied as he held up his empty glass.

Fifteen minutes later, David was beginning to feel a little lightheaded from the three drinks he had consumed in the past forty-five minutes. His head was beginning to hurt slightly from the combination of alcohol, and the constant numerous, disturbing thoughts that seemed to be crushing against his brain. The envelope in his possession contained undisputable, incriminating evidence against his lifetime acquaintance and business partner. Still, he kept trying to find a justifiable reason why Craig would screw him.

David glanced at his watch and wished that he could speed up the flight. The plane had been airborne for three hours. It was nine p.m. The flight was scheduled to arrive at John F. Kennedy International Airport in an hour and fifty minutes. For lack of anything better to do, he decided to take a nap. He pushed the button releasing the back of the seat, leaned back, closed his eyes and drifted to sleep.

The flight attendant's voice over the intercom woke David from his nap.

"We will be landing in New York in just a few minutes. At this time, the captain has turned on the no smoking sign. We ask that you extinguish all cigarettes, and return your seats to the upright position. Please fasten your seat belts and remain seated until the plane comes to a complete stop in front of the terminal. Once the captain has turned off the seat belt sign, you may begin exiting the plane. We hope that you have enjoyed your flight with us, and that you will fly with us in the future."

David sat erect in his seat rubbing the corners of his eyes with his fingertips while looking out the window. Although it was dark outside, he recognized several landmarks. The Triboro Bridge was clearly visible to the left. As the plane swung to the right, while making its final approach to the runway both the Throgsneck and Whitestone Bridges could be seen. All three bridges stood out, outlined by strings of bright lights. The light from the headlights of the cars moving swiftly across the three bridges, created an illusion of a continuous flowing stream of light.

David looked around the plane at the other passengers. It

wasn't too hard to spot those who were flying into New York for the first time. They were the ones turning their heads from side to side, stretching their necks to the limit. They were all goggled eyed while looking out the windows trying to see as much of New York's magnificent skyline from the air as they could.

Paul rested his head against the back of the seat, and became lost in his thoughts once again. 'I hope the limo is waiting. I'm tired. I just want to get home to Sandy. I'll confront Craig tomorrow.'

David had been so distraught upon receiving the documents that he left San Diego as soon as he could book a flight to New York. He told his secretary to phone ahead, and arrange for a limo to pick him up at the airport. He told her not to tell anyone where he was heading. All he wanted was to get home as quickly as possible, take Sandy into his my arms, and hug her until the sun rose the next morning. He always found comfort and a sense of peace in her arms. She represented the one thing that he always considered consistent in his life. Never in his wildest dreams could he imagine the surprise that awaited him at home. His thoughts of arriving home and being with his wife faded as the wheels of the giant jet touched the ground, slightly jolting the aircraft.

Ten minutes after touching down the plane taxied down the runway to a complete stop in front of the main terminal. A few minutes later, one by one the passengers began to disembark from the aircraft.

David remained in his seat watching as several of his fellow passenger walked by, heading to the exit. Seeing a break in the flow of exiting passengers, he quickly climbed out of his seat, reached into the overhead compartment and removed his single piece of luggage.

After exiting the aircraft he casually strolled through the tunnel, leading to the waiting area, where he spotted a man dressed in a navy, blue suit holding a large white placard with "**Jordon**" printed across it in bold letters. David walked to where the man had positioned himself.

"I think I'm the person you're looking for."

The chauffeur lowered the sign and spoke.

"Good evening, Mr. Jordon. Your ride is out front. Can I help you with your luggage?"

"No thanks."

David held tightly onto his briefcase and carryon bag and followed the driver outside.

When they reached the waiting limo, the driver opened the rear door. David bent slightly, stepping inside and eased into the seat. After shutting the car door the driver preceded to the driver's side, climbed in and started the engine. He turned around and pushed the switch that controlled the partition separating him from David until it disappeared. "My office said that you would be going from the airport straight to your home. Is that still your wish, sir?'"

"Yes. Do you know the address?"

"Yes sir. Number twelve, Greentree Road in Brookville."

"That's correct. Do you know how to get there?"

"I sure do. You just sit back and relax, sir. I'll have you safely home in no time at all. If you would like a drink, the red button on the panel to your left will activate the bar. The green one will turn the television on. If you need anything else, just push the blue button on the panel." The driver turned around, and pressed the switch again, shutting the partition. After adjusting the mirrors, he pulled slowly away from the curb, and headed for the expressway leading to Long Island.

The dark, blue limousine cruised east on the Belt Parkway until the driver spotted a sign with arrows pointing in different directions. One arrow pointed to the right for the **Southern State Parkway-Eastern Long Island**. The second one pointed left for the **Cross Island Parkway and Whitestone Bridge**. The chauffer lowered the partition once again and addressed David.

"Excuse me, sir. Would you prefer that I took the Southern State or the Northern State?"

"Take the Southern State to the Meadowbrook North, then the Northern State."

"Yes, sir."

The driver closed the partition again and continued east, while David mixed another drink before pushing the button that controlled the television turning it on. The news was on and just as he expected, the topic was the ever-evolving world crisis. The newscaster was reading an update on the days events, both in The United States and abroad. Suddenly, the reporter ceased speaking and reached for a paper that someone off camera was thrusting at him. He read the message that was just handed him, paused for a second, cleared his throat, and began to speak again.

"I have just been handed a bulletin, which I am delighted to share with you. After three days of non-stop negotiations, the United States has been able to work out a compromise with terms acceptable by all parties to the crisis the world has been faced with. As per the agreement, the Chinese have agreed to release the Russian servicemen taken captive last Friday.

In return, the Kremlin said it would hold a newscast to be televised worldwide. They would apologize for the downing of the Chinese aircraft. They would claim that a software error in their defense system had provided the wrong coordinates as to over whose airspace the Chinese plane was actually flying. They would say that, in actuality, the Chinese jet was precariously close to Russian airspace but had not actually entered it. The arrangement called for the transfer of the Russian soldiers to an undisclosed U.S. military base in West Germany where they would receive a complete and thorough medical exam before being flown to Russia.

Both sides have agreed their military forces on adjoining borders would remain in place and placed on a lesser alert until an additional agreement can be worked out that would prevent a repeat of last week's events.

The President's Press Secretary has announced that the President has scheduled a press conference for nine-tomorrow morning. We will be reporting live from the Oval Office, beginning at eight-forty five."

He was about to turn the television off when the newscaster began speaking again.

"I have just been handed another note by my producer. Talks have ceased between the Chinese and Russians. No reason has been provided as to why the talks were so abruptly canceled. We are told that a short while ago in a television broadcast to his nation, the Chinese Premier announced there would be no further talks with the Russians until they admitted that they deliberately entered Chinese airspace and shot down their planes without provocation."

David's first reaction to the latest news update was to wonder if it was a real bulletin, or just another one of the multitude of fake news reports that had become common over the past few months. Tablets, computers and other electronic devices were being bombarded with unrelenting fake news reports. Thanks to artificial intelligence some of the reports contained images that seemed incredible real to the average person. These fake reports caused panic on multiple occasions around the world.

Governments warned citizens not to react to news reports generated over electronic devices. People were told to check news reports as they aired live on conventional news media as opposed to those they viewed on their personal electronic devices.

People rapidly grew weary of trying to figure out which news was real or which was a deep fake. 'Who was to say that the so-called live conventional news reports being aired were real or also deep fakes,' became the mind-set of millions and millions people globally. Untold numbers of people worldwide began to ignore the news completely and went about their daily lives as if there wasn't a mounting global crisis.

"It will blow over just like the U.S.-Russian crisis," David muttered to himself as he clicked the remote control turning off the television. He made himself another drink before leaning back comfortably in his seat. In reality, the news concerning the Chinese and the Russia concerned David more. He was, however, at the moment, more concerned about his partners' betrayal.

CHAPTER FOURTEEN

The multitude of outside lights outlined the large ranch house on Greentree Road. David and Sandy had purchased the house twelve years ago. It was much smaller then. Over the years, they added several rooms, and installed an Olympic-sized swimming pool out back. Sandy considered herself to have a special knack for interior decorating. Much of her free time over the years had been devoted to decorating and redecorating their home. It was indeed a showplace. The three acres surrounding the house could have been taken from the cover of Home and Garden Magazine. It was impeccable manicured with rows and rows of bright colorful roses and various other flowers all around.

Sandy entertained at their sprawling home frequently, especially during the summer. Everyone who knew Sandy and David, thought of them as the perfect example of a happy, successful couple who enjoyed the fruits of their labor. Never in their wildest dreams could anyone begin to imagine what went on in the house when David was out of town. This evening was no different.

His beloved wife and his partner had been carrying on a love affair for a number of years.

Sandy had secretly lusted Craig since high school. One evening, shortly after Craig's wife passed away, five years ago, he was at home feeling depressed and sad. He knew that David was out of town, and he needed someone to talk to. He called Sandy, told her that he was feeling somewhat down in the dumps, and just needed to talk for awhile. Sandy suggested that he come over, telling him that he would feel much better after they shared each other's company for awhile.

It had taken Craig less than fifteen minutes to make the drive from Garden City to Brookville. Sandy greeted him at the door, instructed him to show himself to the living room, and told that she would join him shortly.

A few moments later she entered the living room dressed in a sexy low cut dress accentuated by black stilettos. Before the night was over, she had succeeded in seducing him. Since that day, they took full advantage of every opportunity they could to satisfy their mutual lust.

Tonight was no different. Cardinal desire was in full swing. David continued to fondle Sandy as she teasingly began to bare her desirable body, garment by garment. First she slowly pulled her top off letting it drop to the floor. Craig's hands roamed ever so slowly over the spongy fullness of her breasts. Sandy began to squirm on the sofa as her lover started tracing the full length of her body. Their mouths were locked together in a wet, passionate kiss, as they slid onto the plush carpet. Soon all their clothes were stripped away and piled in a tangled heap on the floor next to where Sandy was sprawled on her back with her lover laying on top. Sandy began to move rhythmically and moan softly as Craig continued to explore her body. Their bodies twisted and turned almost continuously as they continued with their passionate lovemaking. Suddenly Sandy's buttocks began quivering. Her back arched upward and her entire body shook uncontrollably as she experienced an intense orgasm. Craig soon followed suit with one of his own.

As soon as he caught his breath, he slowly rolled off of her onto his side next to her, arms and legs intertwined. The two lovers remained locked in each other's arms for a long time before separating.

Finally, Sandy rolled onto her side and rested her head in her hand. Craig laid back and closed his eyes. Sandy let him rest for a few minutes, then sprung to her feet. The sudden motion startled Craig, causing him to quickly sit up. Sandy reached for his hand, and playfully tried to pull him to his feet. Craig willing stood and pulled her close to him. They locked in an embrace, and shared another long, wet, passionate kiss. Sandy was first to break the kiss. She took a step back and flung her hair to the side and over her shoulder.

"Grab the champagne, a couple of glasses and follow me."

Before the words had fully escaped her mouth, she turned her head in the direction of the bottle of bubbly on the table. Craig picked up the bottle and two glasses. Sandy grasped his free hand and led him out of the living room, stopping momentarily to dim the lights in the room. Together they slowly climbed the stairs leading to the bedroom. Halfway to the top, they paused as Craig leaned slightly and planted a series of kisses on Sandy's neck, ears, cheeks and lips before inserting his tongue into her anxiously awaiting mouth. Sandy ran her sharp, painted nails gently up his naked skin. They continued up the steps, mouths locked together. When they entered the bedroom, Sandy instructed Craig to pour some champagne and turn on the stereo.

"I'll be right back with a little surprise for you," she whispered before disappearing into the bathroom.

Craig had no idea what was in store for him and wasted no time in following her instruction.

Craig was sitting on the edge of the bed when Sandy returned. She sashayed to the stereo and turned the volume up, almost to its maximum limit. The sound of Chopin engulfed the room. She teasingly strutted back to the bed, stood in front of Craig with an evil grin spread across her face and spoke. "Tell me what you like."

Before he could answer, Sandy was on her knees on the floor in front of him and began kissing her way up his legs. She continued methodically kissing him until he could take no more and began grunting. Finally, she pulled back, stood up, untied the two strings of her negligee and let it drop to the floor. She stepped closer to Craig, until her breasts were directly in front of his mouth. Her teasing was too much. Craig stood up and pulled her tightly into his arms. His chest pressed ever so tightly against her breasts, squishing them lightly. They stood there for a few minutes, holding each other.

Once again Sandy began to tremble with renewed excitement when Craig pulled away while sliding his hands down the sides of her breasts and hips until he reached her buttocks. He gripped her plump, luscious butt cheeks firmly, lifted her off the floor, and laid her gently on the bed. In seconds, they were lost in uninhibited love making; the outside world drowned out by the blaring sounds coming from the stereo.

The two lovers had no idea that David was less than a mile from the house. As the limousine exited the parkway, David began instructing the driver.

"Turn left at the stop sign, then continue straight until you reach the fork in the road. Bear right at the fork and make a left when you reach Greentree Road. It's the last house on the left."

Three minutes later, the car rolled to a stop in front of David's house. The driver got out, opened the door for David. "Thank you," David said as he handed the driver a fifty dollar tip.

"Thank you, sir. Have a good night," the driver replied as he climbed back into the limo and pulled away.

Craig had planned to stay the night with Sandy, and parked his car in the garage so he wouldn't arouse the neighbors' suspicions. David stood momentarily in front of his house taking in the peacefulness that seemed to be everywhere. With the exception of the sound of the concerto blaring from the closed bedroom window, nothing else but silence and stillness surrounded the small, impeccably landscaped estate. David paid little attention to the loud music. Sandy often played music with the volume turned up almost to the maximum when she was home alone.

When he reached the top of the steps he punched in the code that unlocked the door. He took extra precautions not to make a sound as he entered his residence. There was a hidden, mean streak in David. He enjoyed sneaking up on his wife and momentarily frightening her. He knew that she hated it, but he got a small kick out of it.

David usually stuck rigidly to his schedule. Craig and

Sandy, never once during their years as lovers, gave any consideration to David's ever cutting a business trip short, and returning home without first telephoning Sandy.

Once inside, David quietly put his bag down. He looked around and noticed the lights were on in the living room. He walked over to the room, reached for the light switch and turned the lights off. He couldn't wait to lock himself in the security and comfort of his wife's tender arms for the remainder of the night.

Meanwhile, Craig and Sandy were still lost in their private world of carnal lust, totally unaware that David was in the house.

"Yes! Yes!" Sandy cried out, as Craig kissed her and rubbed against her thighs. By now, she was wiggling frantically from the pleasure of Craig's lovemaking. She dug her nails deep into his back as he pressed against her, licking and biting his neck until both were on the verge of another orgasm. Their hips were rocking in synchronized, rhythmic motion as they experienced simultaneous, explosive climaxes, while screaming out in pure ecstasy.

Immediately following their sexual release, they hugged. Sandy began to tell Craig about how much she desired to be with him.

"All I can do when David is making love to me is think of you."

Craig stared at his lover for a few seconds before he replied.

"I wish it could be different, but you know as well as I do, there is nothing we can do."

He forced a smile as he spoke. He knew that his plans did

not include her or anyone else. Monday morning, he would be boarding a plane headed for South America, under an alias, never to be seem or heard from again. He began planning his disappearance almost immediately after his wife's death. Every dime he had stolen from the company was waiting for him in a secret bank account in South America. He could have sold his interest in the company. The only problem with that option was that, after he paid taxes on the money from the sale, it would have netted him a lot less than he could embezzled over the years. Deep down inside, it was his way of getting back at David. He secretly hated him for marrying Sandy. They met her at the same time. He was attracted to her just as much as David. But before he could do anything about it, David had began dating her, and eventually swept her off her feet. Craig smiled at his lover, leaned over, kissed her on the forehead and laid back against the headboard.

The two lovers, had no way of knowing that David was in the house and heard them screaming in heated passion just moments earlier.

David stood in the living room dazed, almost as if he were paralyzed, staring wild-eyed at the pile of clothing on the floor in front of him. He didn't want to believe what he was seeing. He screamed silently as he began to shake his head uncontrollably back and forth. "No! No!" he shouted aloud. Suddenly he snapped.

In a zombie-like state, he walked past the pile of clothing, and entered the den next to the living room. Without hesitating, he walked to the desk located at the rear of the room, reached in the top, left drawer and pulled out a forty-five caliber, automatic pistol. Still in a trance like state, he stared blankly at the weapon. Almost as though he had rehearsed it, he reached back into the drawer, removed a loaded ammunition clip, and inserted it in the butt of the gun. He firmly gripped the pistol, slowly placed his hand on the slide and glided it back. He held the pistol with the slide in the open position for a few seconds as he stared at the picture of Sandy on top of the desk. Tears began to roll down his cheeks. He shook his head and blinked his eyes in a vain attempt to stop the stream of tears which had now begun to flow uncontrollably past his cheeks and dripping onto the floor. After a few seconds, he looked up from the picture and released the slide of the gun, sending it home and chambering a round.

Still dazed and in shock by his recent discovery on the living room floor, David headed for the stairs. While walking past the desk, he lifted his wife's picture from atop it and turned it face down. He continued through the living room until he reached the pile of clothes on the floor. He kicked them violently, causing a wallet to fall from the pocket of the pants onto the floor. David bent over and picked it up. He flipped it open, and went into a deeper state of shock when he saw the name on the driver's license that was visible through the plastic window. The moment his saw the name on the license he let out an animal like howl, dropped the wallet, and dashed up the stairs still screaming. His initial scream was so loud and piercing that the two lovers sprang to their feet. They looked at each other, terrified as a sense of utter and complete panic shot through them. Their look of bewilderment and fright turned to one of shock and utter dismay as David flung the bedroom door open. Sandy quickly stepped in front of Craig. She reached for the sheet in an attempt to cover naked body.

"David, I....." Before Sandy could complete her sentence,

David cut her off.

"Why? Why?," he asked rhetorically.

Before either of them could say anything, David raised the pistol, aimed it at his wide-eyed wife and pulled the trigger. The projectile from the gun struck her in the middle of her forehead, lifting her off her feet and throwing her back into Craig, as part of the top of her head peeled away. Craig jumped back as spurts of Shelia's blood splattered over his face and naked body. He fell backwards onto the bed, as Sandy's lifeless body dropped to the floor.

"Why? Why?," David repeated.

Craig slid off the blood, stained bed, dropped to his knees at the foot of the bed, looked at Sandy's body, her brains dangling from her partially torn away head, and pleaded.

"No, David. Please, don't."

Without saying a word, David pointed the pistol at Craig and repeatedly squeezed the trigger firing round after round. He counted each one as they struck Craig. "One, two, three, four..."

All four slugs caught Craig in the chest, sending him jerking backward crashing against the frame of the bed. David watched as Craig's lifeless body slid onto the floor. He walked to where the bullet riddled bodies lay, sat down between the stained corpses, lifted what was left of his dead wife's head onto his lap, looked down at her, and repeated his earlier question. "Why? Why?"

He remained in that position with streams of tears rolling freely down his cheeks. He held tightly onto Sandy's lifeless body for a while longer. Then with a quick motion, he released his grip on her, placed the forty-five against his head and pulled the trigger. The bullet tore through his head throwing it back, splattering pieces of his skull and brains onto the two bodies on the floor. His lifeless body fell between then.

CHAPTER FIFTEEN

The loud ringing of the bells atop the First Methodist Church in downtown Ramsey had aroused Paul from a deep sleep. For the better part of an hour, he lay in bed staring up at the ceiling, recollecting past events. Two weeks had passed since he read about the scandalous, double murder and suicide in a small town on Long Island, New York. As usual, he was surprised at how the demon finish what he started. Suddenly, Paul felt a sharp pain in his chest. He lifted himself up in the bed, braced his back against the headboard, and coughed several times in rapid succession. He held his hand to his chest, reached for the glass of water on the night table, and began sipping the liquid slowly in an attempt to cool what felt like an intensely hot fire engulfing his entire insides.

For the past two days, he had gotten out of bed only to use the bathroom and to refill the pitcher he had on the night stand with fresh water. He took a guess at what was going on with him. He concluded that he had developed a bad case of pneumonia. It was obvious to those who saw him earlier in the week, that he was a very sick man.

Monday, he met with his attorney to sign the documents

he had instructed him to draft. When they were finished the task at hand, Larry pleaded repeatedly with his client and long-time friend to let he take him to the emergency room of the nearest hospital and find out was wrong.

"Nonsense, it's only a cold. I appreciate your concern. I'll be fine after a few days rest," Paul responded.

Paul knew better. He had wrestled with pneumonia more than once and was keenly aware of the symptoms associated with the disease. He knew that his illness had progressed to where, if he did not seek immediate medical attention he would pay the ultimate price. He had no intention going to a doctor or hospital. Larry didn't believe Paul's feeble attempt to convince him that he would get better without the much needed medical attention that was clearly evident based his condition.

For several days, Larry had been extremely concerned about Paul's health, both physically and mentally. He was literally taken by surprise by Paul's requests of him when they met in New York the prior week. He argued with his client and questioned the sanity of what he was proposing.

"As your friend, I think that you should take a long vacation, and think about what you're asking me to do."

Paul made it as abundantly clear that he knew exactly what he was doing. They bickered back and forth for a few minutes, until finally, Paul snapped at his attorney.

"I said I know what I'm doing. Now are you going to take care of it, or do I have to find someone who will?" Larry threw up his hands in a gesture of frustration. "Bottom line, I work for you. If that's what you want done, I'll see to it. I should have everything ready for you to sign in a couple of days."

"Give me a call when the papers are ready for my signature. We can meet at Delvecheos in White Plains. It's been a long time since we've eaten there, hasn't it?"

"Cool. I look forward to it."

"I'll give you a call when the documents are ready. We can arrange a time then," Larry replied, while forcing a smile.

The strained tension could be felt as the two long-time friends stood up, shook hands and bade each other goodbye.

When they met days later, as scheduled, it was more than obvious that Paul was in worse condition then when they met earlier in the week. His eyes were puffy. Snot was running freely down his nose. He was sniffling and coughing continuously. Seeing Paul in that state raised new concerns in his attorney's mind. Larry once again vigorously pleaded with Paul to let him take him to the hospital.

Paul flatly refused the suggestion. They argued for a few minutes longer before Larry finally gave up trying to convince Paul to seek medical attention. He decided once again not to pursue the subject any further.

Larry carefully went over each document he had prepared for Paul. As soon as he was through reviewing the papers they left and headed to the restaurant as previously planned,

They arrive at the restaurant a short while later. After being seated and ordering a light meal, Paul went over the documents with Larry in order to insure that everything was as just as he wanted it. After reassuring himself they were written exactly as he had requested, Paul signed the papers. Larry asked the owner of the restaurant, whom they knew well, to witness the signature.

Once the formalities were completed they engaged in casual conversation, reminiscing about past times before undertaking the drive back to Paul's home. Immediately after arriving home, Paul thanked his attorney once again before bidding him a goodnight. Ever so slowly and obviously in a great deal of pain, he entered the house and proceeded upstairs where he climbed onto the bed. He had to exert a great deal of energy in order to seat himself erect in the bed. Once upright, he placed two pillows between his back and the headboard, and pulled out a folder containing his copy of the papers he signed earlier. He reached back to the table, picked up his reading glasses and slid them onto his nose. As he was putting them on, his body wrenched in almost unbearable agony from a series of sharp pains that began shooting through his chest.

As quickly as it struck him, the unexpected pain subsided. Once he felt sure that whatever just went on inside his chest had passed, he began to scan the documents on his lap to once again reassure himself that everything was in proper order. He began to reflect on what he had done, and his reasons for doing it.

The first document he reviewed, divided his holdings in Marshall Enterprises, Inc. equally between his employees. They had served him and the corporation faithfully for many years. As such, he felt that they deserved to benefit from their dedication and hard work that helped build the company into the giant enterprise it had become.

The second document left his estate in Ramsey to Elizabeth, his head housekeeper. She had had spent most of her adult life working for the Marshalls at their estate. He thought she might get some joy out of owning the place; if only for a short while. He made arrangements seeing to it that all household expenses and real estate taxes were paid for five years. Afterward, she could sell the entire estate if she wanted to, and was free to do what she wished with the proceeds from the sale.

He left the Manhattan townhouse to Mary, his maid and housekeeper at the house, who looked after the place for more than twenty years. He made the same provisions for her, covering expenses, that he made for Elizabeth.

He left his collection of antique automobiles to Brian, the long-time family chauffeur.

A fifth document called for a twenty-five million dollar endowment for the establishment and the staffing of a foundation for the study of peaceful solutions to conflict between neighboring nations.

A sixth document divided most of the remainder of his estate evenly between his other servants.

The last document he signed Monday, established a trust fund to be used to pay Larry's future fees. He wanted Larry to handle all the legal affairs for his servants and the foundation. Paul also made provisions to set aside money to cover any taxes that would have to be paid by anyone because of his generosity.

When Paul first requested that his attorney draft the documents, Larry questioned him about why he was suddenly wanted to rewrite his will, his explanation threw the attorney for a loop.

"Larry, the way things are right now, with the situation between the Russians and the Chinese growing worse with each passing moment, none of us will be around much longer. When the bombs start to fall, I just want to know that I did the right thing."

His strange statement and ensuing cynical laugh drew a blank stare from Larry.

Paul inserted his copy of his Last Will and Testament back into the folder and placed it on the night stand. Almost immediately, he began coughing again. This time his coughing spell lasted a full ten minutes. When he finally stopped, Paul felt a lump rising in his throat. He sucked in and brought the lump of gooey excrement from his throat up into his mouth. He reached for the glass that he had placed on the nightstand the day before. He proceeded to spit the gooey substance into the glass. He examined the lump. It was a combination of mucous and dried blood. He knew that his condition was getting worse by the hour. If left untreated, he would be dead in a day or two, if not sooner.

Paul lay in bed smiling as he thought of his impending death and his soon to be reunion with his beloved Mildred. Although he had not been in contact with the demon since receiving his last assignment, Paul felt confident that the demon would live up to his end of their deal. There was little doubt in his mind that the demon wouldn't take care of the final details concerning his death and reunion with Mildred, just as he had taken care of the final details of his three assignments. He reasoned that death from pneumonia would be far less painless than dying from a nuclear blast or worst yet, surviving the initial blast, only to suffer a slow painful death from radiation poisoning.

After dwelling on that thought for a minute or two his thoughts drifted to the ongoing crisis between the Russians and the Chinese. Between thoughts, he reached for the television remote control. 'How could anyone believe that, if not resolved, the situation between the two countries would not affect the rest of the world? It's amazing how everyone in America has gone back to business as usual once it was announced that Russia and The United States had worked out the issue between them initiated by the unarmed missal incident in Alaska, even though the issues between the Russian and Chinese governments had yet been resolved.

He continued with his thoughts, as he pointed the remote control at the television mounted in the wall on the far side of the bedroom. He turned on the set while glancing at the clock on top of the night table to his left. It was six p.m.; time for the evening news. The newscaster was just finishing her report on the local news. While she summed up the days events, Paul spoke aloud.

"Look at her, cool as a cucumber." He always admired how, no matter what they were reporting, newscasters always appeared to be cool, calm and collected. The volume on the TV was a little low. Paul adjusted it so he could hear more clearly what was being said.

"And now we turn you over to the network news in New York for complete coverage of developing national and international news."

"Good evening America. I'm Rusty Burns, filling in for Bob Johnson, who is standing by live in Washington this evening attending a special press conference that had been hastily called just a short while ago. Prior to coming on the air, I was notified that the press conference was brief and ended just under an hour ago. Before I turn you over to Bob, who's standing by outside the White House, I'll recap the events we reported on our earlier newscast. Less than seven hours ago, Task, the Russian news agency, announced that several Chinese jet fighters, deliberately and unprovoked crossed into Russian airspace, and launched a surprise attack on two unarmed Russian reconnaissance planes, shooting them down. The Russians responded by launching a rocket attack of their own on units of the Chinese army stationed just on the other side of the Russian-Chinese border. The Chinese in turn retaliated by ordering two divisions of troops to cross over into Russia, and secure a airfield five miles inside of Russia.

As of one o'clock this afternoon, Eastern Standard Time, there were conflicting reports from Moscow and the Chinese concerning the fighting that has erupted. At three p.m. we received word that under obligation of a treaty with the Russia, the Vietnamese have launched an attack into Southern China. An hour later the Russian Premier took an unusual step by making an announcement that was televised worldwide. The Premier was brief in his statement, which has stunned rest of the world. Here now are the details of that announcement as broadcasted earlier.

"The Chinese have exactly four hours to pull their troops out of Russian territory or we will retaliate using whatever weapons we have at our disposal to ensure that the Chinese invaders are driven from our Russia and will never be able to attack Russia or anyone else ever again."

"It was brief announcement, that didn't mix words. It was straight to the point. Within minutes of the Russian ultimatum to the Chinese, The U.S. Presidential Press Secretary announced that the President would be holding a press conference of his own at four-thirty p.m. For reasons still unknown, it was announced that the conference would be held behind locked doors and there would be no live television or radio coverage. It was further announced that reporters attending the conference would be confined to the pressroom for an hour after the conference ended. They then would be released, and free to report on the what was revealed at the highly, secret session. With that, I'll turn you over to Bob, who's standing by outside the White House.

The studio cameras switched from the in-house newscaster to the reporter standing just outside the White House alongside a large contingency of other reporters from numerous media outlets, both domestic and foreign and hundreds of curious onlookers.

"I've just come from The Presidential press conference. As you already know, the entire conference was cloaked in secrecy. The meeting ended an hour ago. For reasons still unknown to us, all reporters who covered the meeting, were confined to the room where it took place until a few minutes ago. It was a rather short conference, during which the President read a brief prepared statement announcing that the Chinese were standing firmly by their position that their invasion of Russia was fully justified. As a result of the Chinese attack, Russia has officially declared war on China.

When The President finished his statement, neither he nor his aides would respond to any of the endless, barrage of questions directed at The President from members of the press. We were informed that shortly before the conference began, The President had been informed that the Russians were standing firm by their threat to retaliate against what they called a deliberate and unprovoked attack on Russia by units of the Chinese military. The President then made the following shocking announcement.

"As you know, when I visited China three years ago, I signed several agreements with the Chinese government in the name of the American people. There is no time to go into details, but one of the agreements was a pledge to aid China in case of an attack from their Russian Neighbors."

Immediately following his statement, the President abruptly ended the press conference, and was ushered from the room, shielded by his aides and at least a dozen members of the Secret Service.

There has been a flurry of activities both in and outside the White House since the President finished speaking. Just a few moments ago, Marine One touched down. We have not been unable to speak with anyone in authority. Wait, the President and the First Lady have just exited the White House. They are surrounded by aides and what appears to be at least a dozen Secret Service agents. A few are carrying suitcases and multiple boxes marked top secrets that appear to contain files of some sort."

The reporter and his cameraman quickly headed toward the emerging President, First Lady and a group of Presidential aides. When several other reporters advanced toward the President, members of the Secret Service, who had been escorting the President and his encourage, rushed forward to block their accessibility to him. Several reporters shouted at the President simultaneously as he was quickly whisked to the waiting chopper.

""Mr. President! Mr. President!"

The President pretended that he couldn't hear their shouts as he and his entire entourage were being ushered with deliberate speed onto the waiting helicopter. One reporter turned to the agent who appeared to be in charge and addressed him.

"Could someone tell us what is going on? Where is the President heading?"

The large blades of Marine One began to rotate in preparation for liftoff, almost drowning out the agent's response.

"For reasons of national security, I can't answer that question."

The reporters continued to fire questions at the agent. As soon as everyone was aboard, Marine One lifted off. It's massive rotating blades sprayed the area with a cloud of dust as the helicopter continued to climb and head west.

Paul didn't want to see or hear anymore. It was crystal clear to him what was going on. The President was being whisked off to some secret Military Command facility deep below the earth in Colorado or elsewhere in the Midwest. It didn't take a genius to figure out why.

He picked the TV's remote control, pushed the off button, and flung the gadget across the room. The box slammed into the television screen, cracking it, causing it to explode. Sparks flew from the set, followed by a huge cloud of black smoke.

Paul glared at the cloud of smoke and began cursing aloud. "Where the hell are you? I've kept my part of our bargain. When are you going to keep yours?"

Before he could continue with his burst of anger, a sudden, excruciating, intense pain shot down the entire length of his left side. The jolting pain he was experiencing was followed by an even more intense pains in the center of his chest. His entire body went limp. He grabbed his chest as he fell back onto the bed. Beads of perspiration began to roll freely down his face and body. He released his hold on his chest, grasped the front of his pajamas top and tore it from his body. His heart began beating rapidly and uncontrollably pounding against his chest. Simultaneously with the ever increasing rate of his heart beat, he began experiencing increased difficulty in breathing. Suddenly, the pain intensified. Paul wrenched from the ever intensifying pain, and began to scream out again at the demon.

"I'll get you for this. Where are you?"

Minutes later, he began to experience a feeling that what remained of his life was being rapidly drained from him. He thought back to a conversation he had with the demon during one of their earlier meetings. He remembered the demon's words.

"Every individual retains the right to chose who gets his soul upon death. Even at the last moment of his life, he can choose by simply renouncing one god, and asking the other to accept his soul. Other than for the purpose of declaring a winner in the end of their game, it didn't matter which God had collected the most souls. When the god finally got bored with their game on earth, they will simply have man destroy the planet, ending the game. At that point, all souls will be brought together to have a celebration honoring the winner of their game. Afterward, a new game will begin somewhere in a distant universe."

As the demon's words echoes in his mind, Paul mustered all the strength that he could, and reached for the picture of Mildred that sat on the night table. He lifted his wife's portrait, stared at it for a moment, smiled, and pressed it tightly against his chest. He took one, last, slow look around the room and cried out. "God have mercy on my soul!"

No sooner than the word "soul" escaped his lips, Paul took in a deep, labored breath before slowly exhaling, and closing his eyes.

Once the last bit of life slipped from Pauls' now stilled body, a powerful wind swept throughout the bedroom. Just as it had done on so many previous occasions the demon suddenly appeared. It stood at the foot of the Pauls' bed in all its glory. The wing like structures from his shoulders were fully extended, and its body again surrounded by flames. The demon looked down at Pauls' lifeless body, which suddenly began shaking back and forth with quick jerking motions. The demon stepped back and waited for what he knew was about to occur. Something that few mortal eyes had ever witnessed was about to happen; the freeing of a persons' soul from the body that housed it through the life of the human being .

The demon stood watching as the soul released itself from the body, which had served as a temporary host for so many years. The demon stepped back from the now free soul, as another figure appeared in the bedroom, and positioned itself between the demonic figure and the newly freed soul. The second figure was almost an exact replica of the demon with two exceptions. It's body was not scaly nor was it surrounded by flames.

The two figures faced one another, staring fiercely into each other's bright, red eyes. The demon spoke first. "Step aside. His soul belongs to my God".

The newly arrived figure responded in a deep, commanding voice.

"Have you forgotten the rules completely? Didn't you hear his last words? He made a choice. His soul belongs to my God."

As they continues addressing each other, the figures took several gigantic step back from each other and snapped their fingers. In a flash, a gigantic sword appeared in each of their hands. Without a moments hesitation they raised the swords high in the air above their heads, and charged forward toward each other. Their shinning blades collided in mid-air, causing a deafening, explosive sound that echoed through the entire universe.

The sound was louder than any previous sound ever heard. The clashing of there swords and the deafening sound was immediately followed by the appearance of a huge ball of flame followed by another huge ball of light. Both balls of light shot toward one another from opposite ends of the room. The two balls collided in mid-air, causing a massive explosion as they meshed into one gigantic ball of bright red, orange and yellow flames surrounded by a white light of the most blinding intensity imaginable.

At almost the same speed at which it was created, the brilliant combination of fire and light dissolved, leaving an empty, vast, open, dark space where only seconds earlier there once was a world. Somewhere off in the distance universe a faint sound could be heard...the sound of a newborn baby crying.

THE END